Mack squeezed off a round of sizzling hollow-points

The driver's body was punched back inside the car.

More bonecrushers flashed through the night. Then the dead man's partner called out from the scrub grass nearby.

"Hold it! You move and the woman dies!"

The guy was holding Toby Ranger in a viselike grip, pointing a machine pistol at her head.

Bolan let the Uzi hang free from its lanyard. He unsheathed the big Beretta, setting the selector on single-shot....

D1041784

Other
MACK BOLAN
titles in the Gold Eagle
Executioner series

Mack Bolan's
ABLE TEAM

Mack Bolan's
PHOENIX FORCE

MACK BOLAN

THE EXECUTIONER 47

BOLAN

Renegade Agent

DON PENDLETON

A GOLD EAGLE BOOK FROM

WORLDWIDE

TORONTO · NEW YORK · LOS ANGELES · LONDON

First edition November 1982

ISBN 0-373-61047-5

Special thanks and acknowledgment to
Steven Krauzer for his contributions to this work.

Printed in Canada

He who does not punish evil
commands it to be done.
> —*Leonardo da Vinci*

When he is afraid,
man is a very vicious being.
> —*Krister Stendahl*

Terrorists say, he's only one man—
we can nail the bastard. And again
and again they are wrong. For I have
no fear. I have given my soul and
my guts to my country and its people,
and my command is clear—to punish
evil with firepower unrelenting.
> —*John Phoenix (Mack Bolan)*
> from his journal

Dedicated to a man betrayed—Police General Carlo Alberto Dalla Chiesa, coordinator of the rescue of U.S. General James Dozier from his Red Brigades kidnappers, who was killed with his bride of two months in an ambush in Palermo, Italy. Chiesa was Italy's top anti-terrorist police officer, and he was felled by the treachery of a close collaborator. The war is indeed everlasting.

PROLOGUE

Mack Bolan stood immobile in the darkness of the New England night. He was listening to the voices of the past.

Before him the slow-moving waters of the Concord River lapped at its banks. Behind him stood a man.

The man wore a rolled-brim hat, a leather jacket with tucked-up sleeves, trousers of homespun. A thong around his left shoulder held a powder horn, its tip sealed with a cork. In his right hand was a long-barreled flintlock musket, primed and loaded and tamped. This was a man who would live free or die.

Mack Bolan turned to regard the bronze figure and murmured, "Live large, Brother." For yeah, this man and the others he represented were indeed brothers of the man known as the Executioner, brothers in soul and spirit, the kinship sanctified in blood and gunpowder, the bond spanning two centuries and a great nation's history.

The date was September 26, 1774, when the citizens of the Massachusetts hamlet of Concord resolved at their town meeting *that there be one or more Companys Raised in this Town by Enlistement, and that Said Company Stands at a Minute's Warn-*

ing in Case of an Alarm.'' Could those people have known that these Minutemen, as they came to be known, would be the vanguard in the war for American independence?

The warm night breeze whispered the words of Minuteman Captain John Parker to Mack Bolan's soul: "Stand your ground. Don't fire unless fired upon, but if they mean to have a war, let it begin here!"

It was a hard and brave philosophy. Its application had not changed in the intervening two hundred years. Mack Bolan did not seek war, but he was for certain being fired upon, along with every other man and woman who cherished the freedoms that those soldiers of the long ago had fought to establish.

The enemy then was the British Redcoats, whose ideologies were nationalism and empire. Today the enemy was the international terror-mongers, incomparably worse, whose ideologies, indefensible and altogether from another age, from now, were enslavement, torture, death.

In front of Bolan, the narrow deck of the old North Bridge reached across the river. Here it had begun. Here, on April 19, 1775, four hundred Minutemen had faced and repulsed the hated Lobsterbacks. Dispirited, discouraged, hurting, the British retreated toward the safety of Boston. By the time they reached Meriam's Corner, a mile east of Concord, they believed they had made it. They sighed their relief, and thinking themselves secure once more, marched on.

Instead they walked into a hellground.

Without warning the woods exploded. The flash of primer, heavy reports of musketfire, made dense clouds of black powder smoke that drifted on the still midday air.

Heavy .75-caliber lead balls tore through Redcoat flesh.

White with fear, hovering on the brink of wild-eyed panic, the British tried to return fire—but there was nothing to shoot at. The Minutemen had melted back into the forest like specters.

Mack Bolan smiled grimly in the darkness. He heard the boom of gunfire, saw the soldiers marching on through the countryside, their red wool uniforms drenched with sweat despite the spring coolness, terror marching at each man's right hand. A tree, a house, a stone wall—anything big enough to hide a man and a musket could spell death.

Yeah, the Redcoats had learned the same lesson that Mack Bolan was teaching the human predators of the twentieth century: how the icy touch of dread really felt when the oppressor turned into the oppressed. The feel of that bony finger along the spine.

And so began the American Revolution. In its parts it was a war like any other war in warrior man-kind's history, filled with pain and death, heartache and futility. Yet from it arose a greater nation than had ever before existed.

Those "embattled farmers" of the past, those citizen-soldiers, had not asked for war. But when it became the only way to stand up for their rights as free men, they did what must be done.

Mack Bolan could do no less than fight to preserve that same nation, that idea, that kind of war.

He stood upon the hallowed ground and listened to the night-voices speak of goodness and truth and independence, and he felt a kinship with the past.

A night-voice whispered, "Good hunting, Brother."

Bolan turned and looked up to the Minuteman on his pedestal. Then he turned again and slipped into the shadows, drawing the night around him like a protective cloak.

1

"Clear," Bolan said in a low voice.

Herman "Gadgets" Schwarz went past him in the darkened hallway and crouched in front of the solitary inner door.

Bolan followed, his sneakered feet sinking soundlessly into deep-pile carpet. This was the upper floor of the two-story headquarters and laboratories of a company named DonCo. Half-hidden in the piney woods off of Route 128, which ringed Boston, neither the building nor its name was particularly well known to the general public; if they thought of it at all, it was as just another electronics outfit along technology row. But, in fact, DonCo was one of the most successful and well-regarded hi-tech think tanks in the country.

Bolan pulled a high-intensity narrow-beam penlight from a belt pouch and clicked it on, focusing the arrow-thin ray of illumination on the lock set flush into the door. Gadgets leaned closer, ran sensitive probing fingers over its surface. "Yale type," he muttered. "Double acentric cylinders, shielded tumblers." He looked up at Bolan. "One of your so-called unpickables."

"Can you take it?" Bolan asked.

Gadgets grinned in the dim light but did not answer. He was already unzipping a flat leather case the size of a pocket calculator, removing a delicate-looking wire-thin instrument.

Mack Bolan had no doubt that Gadgets could "take" the lock; the cool, painstaking Able Team member had not come by his nickname lightly. He had already performed technological magic several times this night—and the hard part was still to come.

This was a softprobe only, a nighttime penetration for purposes of surveillance and intelligence. Although both men wore concealing blacksuits and dark cosmetic goop on hands and face, neither carried lethal weaponry. The only people they might conceivably encounter within the bowels of the think tank tonight, Saturday, would be security guards, innocent folk completely unaware of DonCo's dark underbelly—noncombatants, whom Bolan had no intention of drawing into his war.

The immediate mission required that their presence go totally undetected by all means, both while in progress and after execution. If their tampering were later discovered, all would be for nothing.

From the earliest days of his war against the Mafia, Mack Bolan was aware of the parallel existences of law and expediency. His respect for law was second to no man's. Yet he knew full well that expediency must rule when the ponderous workings of law conspire, however innocently, to protect a traitor's yellow hide.

Bolan heard the soft *snick* of tumblers falling into line. "Got it, Sarge," Gadgets murmured. "I think."

The Executioner flicked off the penlight as Gadgets replaced his lockpick and straightened.

"Wired for backup?" Bolan suggested.

"No," Gadgets said firmly. "That I'm sure of."

Still, Bolan tensed as he palmed the brass doorknob. A remote alarm sounding off somewhere would be disastrous for absolute sure.

Yet there was no other man Bolan would have chosen for this mission than Gadgets. Stony Man One could afford to place his fate and the fate of the entire Stony Program in the wizard's sensitive hands. Gadgets Schwarz had first proved his skill when he bugged a VC command bunker to gain intelligence from a Bolan-Zitka sniper-team operation. Ever since, this rare individual, crafty and nerveless, had been an eager recruit to the blitzing warrior's Death Squad, later to the fight against international terrorism as technical consultant to John Phoenix's Stony Man Farm, and as full-time member of the group's tactical squad, Able Team, secret heroes of three recent missions of unusually blazing intensity.

The legitimate business of DonCo was technology; it followed that its security system was of the latest state-of-the-art design. Although only a handful of people were authorized to know it, DonCo had recently been at the forefront of ongoing sensitive applications studies of the U.S. Navy's newest sea-to-ground missile guidance systems. Every step had been taken to guard against just the sort of covert infiltration that Bolan and Gadgets were now carrying through.

The security facility at DonCo was proprietary, as

Gadgets had explained to his boss during the pre-probe briefing, and it employed a systems approach. This meant simply that security was on-site, tied in to a basement guardroom, and that the entire plant had been designed with counter-subversion in mind. The glass-and-steel-frame design embodied fixed windows, wired with alarms that signaled breakage, accidental or otherwise; ventilation came from a fail-safed rooftop air exchanger. Every legitimate access was limited to the front door; fire doors on the other three sides opened only from the inside, and sounded an alarm even then.

That much they knew before the probe began. Since, they had also encountered the close-circuit television system monitoring the grounds, the deceptively simple lock on the front door that served as decoy to a break-to-activate electric alarm, and the ultrasonic-wave-propagating equipment that criss-crossed the company's lobby with invisible sound-wave tripwires.

The blacksuits and some nimble footwork defeated the TVs, while Gadgets's sharp eye and some coaxial cable and alligator-clip probes took out the electric alarm. A sweep with a superheterodyne receiver/detector revealed the frequency of the UWP transmitter, and a transistorized feedback device neutralized it without causing a "systems failure" readout in the guardroom.

Mack Bolan was willing to risk both of their lives, and his New War, on the correctness of this analysis by his comrade.

The cold metal of the doorknob turned easily in his

hand. He pushed open the door and stepped into the deeper darkness of the office.

Gadgets was hot on his tail, shutting the door, running his hands swiftly along the jamb, his sensitive fingers searching for yet another device that could knock them out. Bolan heard him breathe out relief. "Clean as a Stony Phone," he grinned.

They were in an outer office, a reception room. It was completely dark. Bolan waited until Gadgets had relocked the outer door, then flicked on his penlight for a quickcheck recon. In the sharp beam and its attendant half light, they scrutinized the decor. The receptionist/secretary's desk was a thick slab of butcher-block hardwood set on stainless-steel legs, with a white leather swivel chair. On the desk were a white-leather-edged calendar/blotter set and a matching appointment book, a white pen in a white holder, a white telephone with three rows of pushbuttons and nothing else. Set to one side on a lower table with two drawers was a computer terminal with a video display tube. There was a file cabinet against one white wall, a white sofa with two matching chairs, and a couple of coffee tables on which magazines were arranged in neat overlapping rows. The only real color came gloomily from a couple of abstract framed paintings that looked like microcomputer schematic.

Gadgets was already checking out the door set into the wall behind the desk. The intelligence reports that had gotten them this far had the room beyond as the private office of Frederick Donald Charon—president of DonCo, theoretical scientist with a PhD in cybernetics, mathematics, and computer applications, and holder of an NSC Priority-One clearance.

Charon was an extraordinary man, for sure—with, perhaps, merely a single flaw.

The guy was guilty of treason.

Back up a bit. As was common knowledge, over half the staff of the Soviet embassy in Washington were intelligence agents under direct control of the KGB. One of these agents, a medium-ranker named Tuholske who worked in the legal counsel's office, had secretly defected years earlier. Though hardly privy to everything that went through the embassy, he was occasionally able to pass on some interesting tidbits for the U.S.

Not twelve hours earlier, Tuholske had reported to his control that he had encoded a message to the Kremlin reporting one Frederick Donald Charon offering to sell some unspecified but highly classified defense information for a great deal of money. Was Moscow interested?

Probably. Washington sure as hell was.

The fact that the intelligence was, in fact, three weeks old was unfortunate but unavoidable. Tuholske was under strict orders to make contact only on a rigidly randomized monthly schedule, as a precaution against his being discovered. What made things more difficult, more urgent, was that Charon's present whereabouts were unknown, and inquiries through normal channels had been uniformly stonewalled by DonCo personnel.

This softprobe, therefore, had two purposes. One was to secure hard evidence of Charon's evident treason. The other was to discover his whereabouts, hopefully in time for a regular field agent to interdict the scientist before he could carry through on his offer to the Russians. And the key to both goals was behind that locked door.

A quick little shimmer tingled the Bolan spine. He stood relaxed in the dark zone, but alert, legs apart in his skintight combat blacks and soft black shoes. He watched in the darkness now, taking position in the very background of the gloom as the wizard played his own penlight over a panel set into the wall next to the entrance to Charon's office. The panel held a keyboard, and above it an LED display.

"Automatic access-control system," Gadgets said. He punched a digit at random. It appeared in the display. Gadgets hesitated, punched another, then a third, fourth, and fifth. Next to the five figures the display began to flash "ERROR," like an accusation. Gadgets hit the "clear" button and the display returned to darkness.

"Exactly one hundred thousand possible code combos, pal, Colonel Phoenix, sir!" Gadgets smiled. Then his brows knit in concentration as he made rapid mental calculation. "It would only take us maybe 28 hours to go through them, hitting one a second." He shook his head to himself. "There's another way, though, Sarge. Risky, but—"

"But we're this far into the cold damned chamber," quietly finished the warrior. "Let's play it."

Gadgets was already unzipping his military chestpack, eagerly plucking tools and instruments from its interior.

Two Philips-head screws held the panel to the wall. "Charon is using a number-code system, which tells us that other people besides him have access to his office," Gadgets whispered as he went to work on them. "If he were the only one, he'd use a voice-activated circuit, or a thumbprint reader."

The panel came free and Schwarz placed it on the carpeting, set the screws carefully in the holes. "That could mean other people have access to his terminal, maybe even his user code. If so, it makes life a lot easier for us.... Uh-oh.

"Command decision time, Sarge. The numbers just stacked up against us. In a big way."

Beneath where the panel had been, Bolan saw a circuit board covered with microcomponents and a second one with two parallel vertical rows of ten terminals. To each of these terminals on the second circuit ran a wire coded in a different colored insulation.

"Here's what you have to know, Sarge," Gadgets said. "This is essentially a simple device. When the circuit reads the correct five-digit code, it trips a relay. The relay trips a breaker, the breaker completes a circuit, the circuit activates a mechanical delock. So all you have to do is hotwire the code reader—make it *think* the right code has been punched in."

Gadgets pointed to one of the vertical rows of terminals. "That means clipping a wire from one of these—" he indicated the other row "—to one of these. The only question is, which pair?"

"And if you come up with the wrong answer?" Bolan asked in a voice like blighted night.

Gadgets wiped a sleeve of his blacksuit across his forehead. "It'll blow our heads off. It's trip-rigged."

Mack Bolan's decision made itself. "All right. It goes that way sometimes. Now let's pull. . . ."

"Sarge," Gadgets cut in. His voice was soft, but there was no weariness in it, the assurance was full and rich. "I can crack it."

In Gadgets Schwarz's statement there was no tentativeness. It was a simple expression of fact.

The lighted numerals of the chronometer on Bolan's left wrist read 0132:30 A.M. He gave Gadgets the go-ahead with a nod, said "Mark," and turned away. His respect for this fighting man seemed to resound in the silence. He smiled calmly. Behind him there was no sound as Gadgets studied resistors, transistors, capacitors, detonator—the components of the accesser.

The filing cabinet against the wall was locked, and Bolan did not try to force it. Little of interest would be kept on paper in a company like DonCo. Like at World Fi Cor, tortured hellground of one of Gadgets's and companions' most withering superfast hits, there would be little data kept on paper here. Hard intel would exist as a matrix of electromagnetic configurations on a storage disk in the mainframe of the firm's computer.

To turn any of that into a video display, or a paper-copy printout, a guy needed access to a terminal. For a start. Also needed: user code words, file numbers, likely a number of other cross-references and number-groups. Only then would the logic-machine bare its microchip soul to scrutiny.

If Gadgets Schwartz could get into Frederick

Charon's office, into his computerized crucible there, *if* he could tap in to the DonCo president's personal terminal, *if* Charon's personal access data could somehow be divined, then Stony Man Farm would be in the equivalent position electronically of having a direct line to the man's innermost secrets. Just like that.

Those are the secrets of a man actively involved in selling out his country to the Hounds of Hell.

The drawers below the secretary's computer terminal were filled with pens, paper clips, stationery, a Dictaphone, couple of unlabelled tapes, tools of a secretary's trade. The wastebasket beside the desk held a lipstick-stained butt from a mentholated filter cigarette, nothing else.

It was the white leather-edged desk blotter that yielded paydirt.

With the exception of a few weekend dates, nearly every box in the blotter's calendar insert held some sort of notation. At first glance they were hardly revelatory of DonCo's darkest corporate secret. "Semi-mon. rpts due" was penned in on the 15th; "Rvw pension-plan analysis" was scheduled for the 27th; a Middlesex County Commissioner had paid a courtesy call on the third; the purchasing agent for a major retail chain would be in to see about computers on the 30th.

Just what one would expect on the calendar of an efficient executive secretary—along with a careful note of the boss's absences.

On the Saturday a week earlier, Bolan read, "FC dep." Two days from the present, "FC ret."

That was the outline. Within the pages of the leather-bound appointment diary, Bolan found chapter and verse.

On the previous Saturday, Charon had had reservations on Swissair, leaving Boston's Logan International Airport at four in the afternoon, arriving at Cointrin Airport in Geneva at 8:20 the next morning, local time. Beneath that was a memo: "European appointments by private arrangement, next eight days through Monday. No contact except per emer. procedure. Query FRANCOFILE, stand. acc. code."

Bolan paged quickly through the next week. There was no further indication of Charon's activities or whereabouts until the page for the next Monday, little more than twenty-four hours from now. At 9:40 Monday morning, Charon was scheduled to depart Cointrin for Heathrow Airport via British Airways, arriving 10:10 London time. Exactly one hour and twenty minutes later, Charon was supposed to hop a TWA flight back home to Logan.

On the same page of the appointment book, Bolan's penlight beam picked out the reminder, "Brunch with Sir Philip at airport, 10:25, VIP lounge."

For a guy headed from Switzerland to Massachusetts, London was a hell of a sidetrip for the sake of a quick meal.

Bolan scanned the page again, committed every word and number to memory, then flipped the book closed and positioned it exactly where he had found it.

"Sarge!" Gadgets called softly from across the room.

Bolan's chronometer read 0139:10.

Gadgets had clipped one end of a jumper wire to the third terminal from the top of the left row. He held the other end in a steady hand.

"Which one does it connect to?" Bolan asked, reaching for it.

Gadgets grinned in the dimness and shook his head. "This is my gig," he said softly.

He clipped the wire's free end to the top terminal on the right.

For a split second there was no sound at all.

Then there was the click of a deadbolt being drawn back mechanically, and the soft rush of air as Gadgets exhaled his relief.

It took him no more than thirty seconds to remove the jumper, replace the faceplate, return his tools to the chestpack. He stood up and gestured at the door, said, "We did it. You want the honors?"

Bolan turned the knob without a sound and pushed open the door to Charon's office. Subliminal quivers tickled him.

He smelled the snarl, the drooling, guttural, teeth-bared snarl a heartbeat before his flashlight picked out the two bloodred eyes. Bolan's mind whistled, howled, he had only time enough to set himself for the attack.

The satanic eyes rose up toward him and hit him full in the chest.

Bolan went down, but with both hands gripping the Doberman's shoulders. Fetid canine breath expelled into his face. Slavering jaws barked like a mad dog's at Bolan's throat. Teeth snapped shut on nothing but air, though they came so close that Bolan felt the animal's clammy muzzle brush his face. Hot anticipatory dog saliva soaked through the neck of the blacksuit.

Bolan got his left arm around as he lay on the floor and clamped the dog's head against his chest to immobilize the slashing carnivorous teeth. Eighty pounds of steel-wire hound-muscle writhed and struggled to break the hold. The dog's forefoot caught Bolan in the chest, hard enough to take his breath away. A hind paw scrambled for purchase, narrowly missing Bolan's groin. Bolan held all the tighter, pulling the animal's head bone-to-bone against his chest. Then he squeezed with one arm only, at maximum strength.

Fleet fingers from his free hand found the familiar shape of pistol grip. Bolan drew, lay the muzzle against the twisting animal's haunch, pulled the trigger.

There was no recoil, no sound beyond a quick soft gasp.

The dog's maddened snarl turned to a weak growl. He made one final feeble effort to jerk free, then lay still.

Bolan got to his feet. The fight had taken fewer than ten seconds. Gadgets Schwarz stood over the dog, his own pistol drawn.

The weapons were identical: Beeman/Webley Hurricane air pistols. The gun had only the most superficial relationship to the BB rifles that Mack Bolan roamed the woods with near Pittsfield in his youth. The B/W Hurricane was powered by a piston-charged compression chamber that produced 60 pounds of potential energy, enough to spit a .22 slug at better than 400 feet per second. True, this was significantly less energy and velocity than a traditional .22 pistol, but the airgun in the right hands was a potently lethal—and silent—machine.

The Hurricanes that Bolan and Gadgets carried on this softprobe were not designed for killing. Stony Man armorer Andrzej Konzaki had modified them to shoot not slugs, but darts containing a powerful and fast-acting tranquilizer. Originally the guns were to be used only as a last resort, if confronted by a security officer.

Bolan swept his light over the sedated animal. The devouring pinscher was long and lean, black as the blitzer himself. He would not kill an animal if he could help it, even a kill-trained one; it had no place in his war.

Outside in the hallway, someone pounded on the anteroom door.

Bolan flicked off the flash, froze in the darkness.

Silence, then more pounding.

The pounding stopped. The door eased open.

"He's not here." The relief in the man's voice was obvious.

"Of course the mutt's not here. He's in the boss-man's office where he belongs. Let's get moving."

"I say I heard him making strange noises."

"Listen, we got two minutes till we have to punch in at Station Four. I'll go easy on you, you're new. The dog is making strange noises because *any* noise it makes is strange. You ever seen it? If you have, you never wanna see it again. That is a mean pooch, Edgar. I leave him alone, he leaves me alone, we're both happy.''

"I think there's something going on in there.''

"I tell you what, Edgar.'' The older guy was losing his patience. "You have a need to let that hound chew you up into Gainesburger, you go right ahead. Me, I'm gonna punch in at Four.''

There was a pause before Edgar said, "I'm going to check on him.''

Inside Charon's office, Bolan slipped another tranquilizer dart into the Hurricane's breech, cocked the pistol, leveled it on the door.

Footsteps shuffled across the carpet in the outer office. They stopped in front of the access-control panel.

Bolan's eyes etched the darkness as he waited for this non-notable to approach. But then the guard muttered, "Ah, the hell with it.''

Bolan gave him ten beats to get to the outer door and close it, then turned to Gadgets.

"Let's get down to business.''

2

Mack Bolan lit a cigarette and shifted restlessly in the padded leather swivel chair. April Rose, sitting across the conference table from him, caught his eye and flashed him a fast smile. His ally during The Executioner's final Days of De-Creation with which the Mafia wars ended, the tall lush-bodied woman was now "housekeeper" at Stony Man Farm headquarters, overseeing every incredible aspect of the operation, providing logistics, back-up support, care to the few and mighty—to Mack Bolan, Able Team, Phoenix Force—who deployed against the terrorist menace.

This meeting in the War Room was a debriefing.

"The Hurricane worked like a charm," Gadgets Schwarz was saying. "Then, just before we git, I shot the Doberman with the stimulant, and he was already waking up when Mack and I got the hell out of there. From one tinkerer to another, Andrzej, nice work."

"Andrzej" was Andrzej Konzaki, and he was no more a tinkerer than Gadgets. Officially on staff with the CIA, unofficially detached as consultant to Stony Man, Konzaki was one of the most skilled and innovative armorers in the world. As a marine in Vietnam, he'd won a Silver Star—and lost both legs above the knees. But like Mack Bolan, Konzaki saw no profit in living in the past. Now he had the torso of a weight-lifter, the hands and the imagination of an armorer master craftsman. He was to be trusted as *the* expert in every small arm from pistol to heavy machine gun, as well as knife, small explosives, ever more lethally exotic devices.

"Gadgets," Bolan said, "you must brief Aaron on the set-up you rigged to Charon's computer. I want him ready to take over as backup."

Gadgets turned to the fifth person in the War Room, a big rumpled-looking guy hunched over the control board of a computer terminal console that was set up at one end of this operating heart of the Stony Man complex. "DonCo has an in-house mainframe computer, of course, addressable from any terminal in the place," Gadgets explained. "But on Charon's personal terminal, and probably on the terminals of his senior staff, there's a phone link. That allows him to 'talk' to any other phone-linked computer—to exchange data, place or accept orders, whatever—over a regular phone line. You know the technology, Aaron—no point in rehashing the details. But the bottom line is that we're tapped into that phone line."

Bolan stubbed out his cigarette. "What kind of access does that give us?"

"Right now we can eavesdrop," Gadgets replied. "We can monitor and copy anything that is requested from the DonCo mainframe computer, or any computer with which it's linked, if the request comes from either Charon's terminal or his secretary's.

Aaron, I've inserted the access protocol in your file.''

The big man at the console nodded. His fingers danced over the keys. Lines of characters darted across the video display in front of him. He scanned them, typed again. This time, except for a couple of lines at the top, the screen was blank.

"No traffic," Aaron reported.

It was just after five, Sunday morning. The softprobe of DonCo had been completed only three hours earlier. "So until someone uses one of those consoles, those taps don't do us any good," muttered Bolan.

"Not quite, Sarge," Gadgets said softly. "If we can figure out Charon's personal access protocol— his user ID, his query codes and so on—we can duplicate them. From the computer's point of view, we'd be disguised as Charon."

"That's the nice thing about phone lines," Aaron nodded. "They work both ways."

"We already have one lead. That reference to 'FRANCOFILE' you saw in the appointment book," said Gadgets. "It won't get us in by itself, but it's a point in the right direction."

"We'll get on it right away, Mack," Aaron declared. "But I can't predict time frame."

Aaron "the Bear" Kurtzman ruled over the Virginia headquarters' electronic library. In addition to the Farm's own extensive data banks, Aaron could interface instantly with those of the National Security Council, the Justice Department, the CIA, DIA, the intelligence agencies of every major friendly nation. Kurtzman was not simply the operator of this expansive communication and information system; he seemed himself a grizzled, portly extension of it.

Gadgets and Kurtzman began to toss around ideas on how to decode Charon's computer domain. April Rose joined them. Her advanced degrees in electronics and solid-state physics made her no stranger to the arcane mysteries of electronic computation.

In front of Mack on the polished surface of the War Room conference table, in an unmarked file folder, was a digest of the dossier of Frederick Charon. It occupied no more than three pages of sprocket-hole-edged computer paper. Bolan had no need to consult it. He knew the details on those pages well enough. And they told an old and familiar tale.

The salient points were simple: it was the American success story. To a point. Charon was the only son of Italian immigrant parents, his father a self-educated salesman and opera buff, his mother an elementary school teacher. They were dedicated, ambitious people, and they instilled ambition in their son. From Boston Latin High School, Charon went to MIT for his undergraduate work, then Stanford for graduate and post-doctoral programs. His first and only job as an employee was with the prestigious Rand Corporation think tank; when he was twenty-five he left that firm to form his own company, DonCo. In ten years he had built it into one of the most respected theoretical hi-tech firms in the country, and a repository for the country's most profound trust.

And then he chose to betray that trust.

Somewhere along the line, the ambition inculcated in Charon by his hard-working parents had been perverted—into compulsion. A brilliant man, Charon was also brilliantly flawed. No matter what he had achieved—intellectually, socially, financially—he had to have more of everything that fed his will. Perhaps, Bolan mused, his downfall was preordained, as is the defeat of any man whose appetites forever exceed his reach.

Just a few hours before, as he and Gadgets had withdrawn from the DonCo headquarters along the predetermined route that evaded the unblinking TV surveillance cameras, Bolan had stopped to look back at Charon's building. Sleek, low-slung, all tinted glass and polished steel glinting in the starlight, set majestic amid manicured lawns edged with stately woods, it was a monument to the man and a symbol of his failure all in one.

As a scientist, businessman, theoretician, Charon was an extraordinary success, and here were housed the fruits he had nurtured and picked. As a would-be jet-setter, playboy, gambler, profligate, Charon was a failure. His failure was forever compounded by a decision to turn to treachery, perhaps in a vain attempt to salvage the hellbent part of the life he had made for himself.

There was an irony there in which Bolan saw no humor. Charon had achieved the American Dream, in the only country in the world where that dream could still become reality. Then he had turned about and *sold out the country*, had turned the dream into nightmare. Damned cold-eyed thing to do, alchemy in reverse, altogether of the devil's empire, vile, malicious. A prophecy of terror.

"Mack." Aaron Kurtzman's voice broke in. "Communication coming, NSC. It's Hal."

Bolan caught April Rose's gaze, and this time there was no hint of a smile. Communications from head fed Hal Brognola near dawn on a Sunday morning meant only one thing.

In the rare and precious moments they could snatch together, April had made her feelings clear to him. She acknowledged her dedication to the responsibilities that that man had willingly taken on, and confirmed it with her own lifetime commitment to the same cause.

And yet, as she had told Mack Bolan, she was a woman and she was human. Every time he stepped into that arena, she felt woefully incomplete until his safe return.

April nodded slightly, as if in response to his thoughts, and broke the eye contact. Bolan turned to Kurtzman. "Scramble it, Aaron, SOP."

"Already done."

"Thanks. Put it up on video."

"Give me a minute, Mack." Kurtzman went back to his keyboard.

There was more to Bolan's mood than the restlessness of inactivity, plus the anger at a man's betrayal of the country that had given him every opportunity. The brief visit to Massachusetts had awakened other memories as well, memories that Mack Bolan the man could never banish, would never wish to banish.

They were of a time when the wrong people were winning.

Strategists used to refer to a "domino theory" in

discussing the Asian war in which Bolan had fought. But in a town in the shadows of the Berkshire Mountains of western Massachusetts, other dominoes had fallen.

Bolan had seen his personal domino theory quite clearly: there was still, back then, one domino left to fall. And it was he who tipped it over, single-handedly wiping out the gluttonous criminal vipers who had been directly responsible for his personal tragedy.

Earlier in the siege against the bloody Cosa Nostra, Bolan had become aware that, like Vietnam, this would be a war of attrition. The strategy was to annihilate the enemy, first as a means of neutralization, ultimately as a means of destruction of the criminal edifice.

Bolan understood that the war of attrition was now, for John Phoenix, a war of containment. He had no delusions about his own capabilities; Mack Bolan, a.k.a. John Phoenix, was one man, and no one man was going to save a vast impersonal world. But one man, sure, could aspire to fight to keep corners of that world free and green, could push back the corrosive advance of those who would replace freedom with fear, democracy with domination.

The Mafia was a clear and present evil, an entity motivated solely by greed, by the dark side of the herding instinct, in which men mobbed up to commit evil far beyond the capacities of themselves as individuals. Among the ranks of the terrorist brigades, however, there were some who were motivated by misplaced idealism. However inexcusably wrong-headed their ideas of how they would run society, however vicious their damfool methods of imposing their will, Bolan recognized that one in a hundred of these tagmen were dedicated warriors. They just goddamned put themselves in the cross fire. He would have to be careful.

But for the Frederick Charons of the world, Bolan felt no reluctance to curb his blazing powers of attrition whatsoever. He knew that, to the core of his soldier's heart.

"I've got Hal," Aaron Kurtzman called.

On the opposite wall was mounted an oversized 5-by-5 TV screen. It could be used to display computer-generated graphics, maps, charts, photos, or in conjunction with the communication system. On it now, there appeared the imposing, graying figure of Harold Brognola, twice as big as life, slightly distorted by the screen's curvature, and looking grim.

There had been a time when Bolan and Brognola had been adversaries—unwillingly so, but adversaries nevertheless. In that other lifetime of the Executioner, Brognola had been pledged to bring his head in on a pike, even though he was aware that this man had done more to hobble the Mafia hyena in a few years than Brognola's OrgCrime unit had done in decades. After the Las Vegas campaign, however, Brognola the pragmatist took over from Brognola the man, and though cop to the core, he could no longer pursue such a death hunt. By the latter days of the Mafia wars, Brognola was lending active support to the blitzing fighter, and it was he who made the president know that the country need-

ed Mack Bolan in the new wars against the terror-
brokers.

Brognola nodded and said, "Hello, Striker." He
paused, pinching at the bridge of his nose. Bolan
could see the weariness in that good face.

"Frederick Charon," Brognola said finally. "It
turns out he was only the tip of an iceberg."

"If you find the tip, you find the iceberg."

"That's right," Brognola grinned wanly. "And
this is one iceberg we oughta blow right out of the
water."

3

Bolan's chronometer read 1610:30 when April Rose came into his personal billet at Stony Man Farm. He was fully awake before she eased open the door; back in his Vietnam days he had cultivated the facility for combat sleep, had taught himself to relax and recharge the physical and psychic batteries while remaining alert to any signal, any danger or approach.

April was standing just inside the doorway, her fine figure silhouetted by the hallway light. "We've got a wedge in," she announced.

Bolan nodded grimly and arose from the bed. Frederick Charon's computer had finally yielded at least some of its secrets.

"Gadgets and Aaron were working on it most of the day," April told him as they moved down the corridor. "Gadgets was pulled away an hour ago. Able Team has been activated."

Bolan dug the last cigarette from a crumpled pack. As commander of the Stony Man Farm cadres, he always felt tension when his men were called into action.

He thought gratefully of Gadgets. The guy made Bolan smile, even though Schwarz was tougher than nails. He was such a mystery half the time. Believed, from an earlier confession, to have had parents who died in the sixties, Gadgets did in fact have a mother living still, a true eccentric, domiciled with her cats in Pasadena in a distance from reality no less great than the rumor of her death was, which, in her strange and lonely grief, had been her idea to begin with.

Thanks so far, Gadgets. And good luck, great good luck with Able's next one....

The corridor ended at a windowless heavy steel door devoid of insignia. Next to it was a panel containing a one-foot-square glass panel at eye level, a smaller panel at waist level, and a speaker/microphone grill. April looked into the larger panel, placed the pad of her thumb against the smaller, and pronounced her name. The steel door slid noiselessly open, admitting her and her only into a featureless antechamber backed by a similar door.

The corridor door slid shut and a red light blinked on above it, shining for ten seconds or so before going out, indicating April was through the interlock. Bolan repeated her process, pronounced the word "Phoenix" into the mike. A few moments later he was with her in the War Room.

The Bear was at his computer terminal. On the end of the conference table next to him was an ashtray containing his pipe and a scattered pile of computer printouts, most of them dusted with the ash from Virginia's best cut.

"I think we've got something, Mack," Kurtzman said in his deep voice, not turning. He inputted something and watched as characters raced across his video display, then leaned back and grunted with satisfaction.

"Gadgets and I were able to figure out the format of Charon's 'signature.' " Kurtzman turned to Bolan for the first time. "That is, the number of letters and characters and so forth of his user code and access protocol."

"Aaron," April prompted gently.

"Beg your pardon? Oh, right, sorry." Kurtzman stuffed dark tobacco into his pipe. "I tend to forget that computer detective work might not be as interesting to you as it is to me." He touched a match to the pipe, puffed out great clouds of blue smoke.

"Okay, the bottom line," Kutzman said. "Two bottom lines. One—we're not ready to address the DonCo mainframe yet, but we do know that Frederick Charon has juggled the computer books to disguise the fact that a prototype of the new missile guidance system that his company was developing is now missing, along with the specifications manual that he himself developed."

"How big a prototype?" Bolan asked.

"Physically? It would be fairly substantial—it would have to include a control board and a display of some sort. I'm guessing to a degree, but I'd say two standard twenty-two inch bays, each about as tall as a refrigerator. The manual would be no size at all. Reduced to microfiche—which it probably already is—it would fit in a small envelope."

"Okay," Bolan nodded. "What else?"

"Two—something that looks very much like that missing prototype was shipped to Transworld Import/Export, an outfit that has a warehouse in the International Zone at Heathrow Airport in London.''

"That way," April explained, "any cargo held for transshipment only does not have to pass British customs.''

"Third," Kurtzman growled on, "Transworld I/E is a front run by our friends in MI5—British Intelligence.

"And fourth, there is a—" here Kurtzman shuffled through the printouts "—a 99.3 percent chance that this 'Sir Philip' whose name you saw, Mack, in Charon's datebook is Sir Philip Drummond, a high ranking MI5 official."

"Wait a minute," Bolan objected. "That doesn't make sense."

Kurtzman smiled with satisfaction. "It does if you add in point number five." He held up his hand, palm out, all digits splayed.

"Sir Philip Drummond is a puppet," he announced. "And the Kremlin is pulling his strings."

Bolan's coffee cup was still half-full when he left the War Room. Within an hour, he was in a military jet, clearing the Atlantic coast, racing to meet the incoming twilight.

4

The man sitting alone at the corner table was in his mid-fifties, and wore the years well. He was dressed in an impeccably cut Savile Row three-piece suit, gray with muted gray pinstriping, and his full head of silvery hair looked as if it had been styled that morning, every strand in place. He was slim and tall, carried himself with an offhand grace, visible now as he came into the VIP lounge on the first floor of the departures section of Terminal Three at Heathrow Airport, London, England.

From his position four tables away, Mack Bolan had a clear line of sight to the elegant man. Two walls of the lounge were glass, looking out on the airport's terminal aprons. Planes with a variety of international markings taxied to or from the building every minute or so; Terminal Three handled intercontinental traffic. A third wall of the lounge was faced by a long table on which a luxurious buffet brunch had been laid out, a complimentary courtesy for the international passengers that the various airlines were most anxious to woo: business people, statesmen, anyone who did a good deal of traveling. The brunch was presided over by a Pakistani chef in livery, as was the cocktail bar tucked up to the fourth wall.

At mid-morning, there were no more than a dozen people in the room. Of the four at the bar, Mack Bolan knew the identities of three. The sandy-haired man at one end was named Voorhis; the man with whom he appeared to be in deep conversation was named McMahon. Both were American Intelligence agents.

At the other end of the bar, a young blond man, hardly twenty-five, appeared to be dawdling over a Guinness stout.

In fact he was an agent of MI5. Like his American colleagues, he was fully briefed on what was to come down.

The distinguished-looking man at the corner table glanced at his watch, then took a sterling silver cigarette case from his inside jacket pocket. He extracted a slim brown-paper cigarette, produced a lighter that matched the case, drew in flame.

His name was Sir Philip Drummond, and although he did not know it, he was sitting right in the middle of a suck.

A West Indian waiter in immaculate whites approached Bolan's table and refilled his coffee cup. Bolan's protective coloration for this rather refined corner of the human jungle consisted of a lightweight turtleneck and conservative slacks. The coordinated jacket was specially cut to conceal the Detonics mini-.45 Associates automatic pistol riding in custom-crafted shoulder leather under his left arm. On the table next to him was a slimline Samsonite attaché case with combination lock.

Three tables away, Sir Philip stubbed out his half-smoked cigarette and glanced impatiently at the lounge's entrance. He did not smile, but his frown relaxed as he rose from his seat.

Frederick Charon crossed the room.

The two men shook hands with no particular warmth, then both sat down.

Bolan kept them in the corner of his vision. To all appearances, two classier members of a pair of great nations, meeting to discuss something of worth or import within the elegant surroundings to which they had been bred.

In reality, two traitors, pooling resources to sell out those great nations. For all their intelligence, culture, and social status, to Mack Bolan these two men were certainly no less harmful than a pair of fat old Mafia dons who argued obscenely about how to split the profits of their vicious exploitation.

It was all a question of choices. Charon and Sir Philip could have chosen to be leaders, men who enriched the societies to which they had climbed to the top. Instead they had chosen to be criminals.

The clue to the tie-in had come with the notation on the datebook of Charon's secretary: "Brunch with Sir Philip." It was an elementary computer exercise for Aaron Kurtzman: compare that name to all names filed in the Stony Man Farm data banks, with crosscheck to the NSC computer. It had taken exactly 51 seconds—Kurtzman was proud to announce—to produce the correct name.

Bolan had studied the printout summary of Sir Philip Drummond's dossier on his transatlantic flight. Now aged fifty-six, he was the only son of a titled family that traced its lineage back to England's famed House of York. He was a member of the House of Lords, and was third-ranked officer below the Minister of Defence. His private school was Eton, after which he read for his baccalaureate at Cambridge University. In addition he held a Master of Arts degree from Oxford.

And for more than thirty years, Sir Philip had been a double agent for the Russian KGB.

This dignified creep had first become involved with communism as a theoretical system, when he joined a socialist student faction at Cambridge. Such an association was not particularly unusual in those days, was considered no more than a harmless intellectual flirtation. Since Sir Philip had renounced it quite quickly, it was no barrier for his entrance into the British Intelligence service, first as a military officer during the Second World War, then with MI5 after mustering out. That is how the "old school tie" has always worked in England.

In fact Sir Philip had embraced communism totally.

When an old college chum who had already gone turncoat approached him, Sir Philip signed on with the Soviet cause.

For over twenty-five years he rose through the ranks, in the parlance of the trade a "sleeper," an agent-in-place. In carrying out his intelligence duties, he showed only the most scrupulous attention to the best interests of Great Britain.

Then, two years ago, Sir Philip was "activated" by his Russian masters. A deception that had consumed the man's lifetime was finally to bear fruit.

It turned rotten within a month. That was how long it took MI5 to realize Sir Philip was a "mole."

Over the years, British Intelligence has had its share of double agents. The most famous was Harold Adrian Russell Philby, better known as Kim, a Soviet double who rose to become first secretary of the British Embassy in Washington before fleeing to Mother Russia in 1963. Guy Burgess and Donald Maclean were another pair of traitors, escaping only because Philby tipped them off that they were about to be blown.

As a result, MI5 had instituted certain failsafes, one of which had revealed Sir Philip.

Sir Philip himself had no idea that his perfidy was known, because he had been left in place and allowed to operate. He was also unaware that every piece of British intelligence he passed on to the Kremlin was deliberate misinformation, which was all he was still allowed access to.

Today, however, Sir Philip had slipped through to act as go-between for highly classified American defense data, sold to Russia by Frederick Charon. In a few minutes that transfer was scheduled to take place.

"It's why I'm here, guy," Bolan muttered to himself. Present and correct, armed, ready. The Executioner was abroad again.

At the corner table, Charon slipped a hand inside his five-hundred-dollar suitcoat and took out an ordinary letter-sized envelope. Sir Philip did the same. The envelopes changed hands, disappeared into pockets. Sir Philip rose and elegantly crossed the room toward the exit.

The young MI5 agent who had been nursing his stout fell into indiscreet step behind Sir Philip. His name was Lemon, and his nominal assignment was as bodyguard to Sir Philip, as it had been for the past six months. Sir Philip's treason was known to only a handful of people, for obvious security reasons, so as far as Lemon was outwardly concerned, his boss was just what he seemed.

As Sir Philip passed fluidly out of the room, Bolan nodded in the direction of the American agent, Voorhis. He and McMahon moved away from the bar. They were pros for sure. At the corner table, Voorhis said something in a soft voice to Charon. Charon went white, but did not reply. Voorhis spoke again. Charon stood and walked across the room, Voorhis and McMahon flanking him closely. Charon's gait was unsteady.

One down, one to go—as soon as Bolan saw to a further little piece of business.

The Russians were anticipating a package, and they were going to get one—except the contents would not be quite what they expected.

Bolan stood, picked up the attaché case.

Yeah, treason was a risky business. It had a way of blowing up in your face.

Bolan followed the parade through the door.

There was nothing fancy about the hangar that housed the offices, maintenance shop, and warehouse of Transworld Import/Export, the MI5 front through which Sir Philip was transshipping the missile guidance system prototype. It was a corrugated tin building that stood off by itself beyond Terminal One, the Heathrow facility reserved for domestic and European flights operated by U.K. airlines. Facing away from the terminal were double loading-bay doors on rollers; opposite was the entrance.

Bolan watched from the shadow of the terminal as Sir Philip Drummond crossed to the entrance, trailed by Lemon. The Russian mole produced a key-ring and unlocked the pitted metal entry. Electric light flared inside the windowless building, then the door swung shut.

Bolan gave them twenty beats before following. The key he had been provided by MI5 turned noiselessly in the lock. He also came equipped with a neat little .45 Detonics, the cut-down gun so good for concealability.

The inside of the hangar was a single cavernous room, except for a line of offices along one wall. Light showed there behind a frosted glass door. Close up, Bolan could hear the soft murmur of Sir Philip's voice.

Bolan soundlessly eased the Detonics free of leather, raised it head-high and slammed the barrel into the frosted glass.

Sir Philip was seated behind a chipped scarred desk, holding a telephone receiver. He recradled it, looked up at the gun-toting stranger framed by the jagged shards still clinging to the window frame, and murmured fatuously, "I say...!"

The MI5 bodyguard was to Bolan's left, his back to the wall, hands loose at his side, unmoving. He stared at Bolan expressionlessly.

Bolan turned the inside doorknob and came into the office. Glass crunched underfoot.

Without looking in the bodyguard's direction, Bolan said, "All right, Lemon, you know what to do."

From the corner of his eye, Bolan caught the flash of gunmetal.

He whirled, but Lemon had already dropped to a crouch. Bolan started a defensive roll.

Lemon shot him in the left shoulder.

Bolan felt the shock of the bullet furrow into his flesh, but seconds would pass before pain followed.

Only a fraction of the first second was gone when Bolan roared up and struck the youngblood bodyguard.

Lemon fired again, but Bolan's shoulder shoved into Lemon's arm, and the slug buried itself in the ceiling as Bolan's full weight pinned the man in a sprawl against the wall. Lemon tried to get a knee between Bolan's legs. Bolan twisted clear. This time pain lanced savagely through his shoulder.

Then his right hand was free. He smashed the barrel of the little Detonics against the British agent's temple, and the man went down.

Bolan rolled clear. Sir Philip was halfway out of his desk chair.

"Don't." Bolan waved the .45. Sir Philip sat down again.

The body on the floor lay motionless.

Lemon's gun, an Enfield .38 revolver with a two-inch barrel, was still in his outflung hand. Bolan plucked it away, stood, tucked it into his belt.

Because of Lemon's crouch and Bolan's roll, the slug that had hit The Executioner had entered at an upward angle. The exit wound was almost at the shoulder. There was not too much blood. Bolan transferred the Detonics to his left hand, pressed a scrap of the ragged turtleneck over the rear bullet hole with his right.

Even if a guy planned every number down the line, one glitch could throw those numbers straight to hell. Maybe Lemon was a Russian double too. Maybe someone just screwed up, never informed him. But those answers would have to wait.

Sir Philip regarded Bolan dispassionately. Moving slowly and deliberately, he got out his cigarette case and lit up.

Bolan knew the guy had spent a lifetime walking the edge of the knife. The aristocratic polish was simply a superficial shell over a hard and dangerous man.

With the play now on a bloodsoaked heartbeat, Bolan had to show him what hard and dangerous really meant.

"When do the Russians pick up the prototype?" Bolan asked, his voice flat, icy. His left arm refused to cooperate in the simplest action. He applied all his will to ignoring what already felt like it was no longer there.

The Britisher was good all right. The traitor did not bother with any "I-don't-know-what-you're-talking-about" routine. He just shook his head and gave Bolan the merest smile.

Bolan leaned across the desk and levelled the

Detonics into Drummond's face, six inches away. "You broke the rules, Drummond," the Man from Ice said. "But I'll go you one better."

Bolan laid the muzzle of the Detonics on the bridge of the British traitor's nose. "I'm not playing by any rules at all," he said.

The smile washed out of Drummond's expression, and what took its place said the guy had become a believer. Every word Bolan had said was truth and Drummond knew it.

"You're turned up, Drummond," Bolan went on relentlessly. "You are blown. I know, and MI5 knows. Pretty soon your pals in the Kremlin will know. Think they'll like that?"

Bolan knew that Drummond had been around long enough to understand what this meant. Now he was worthless as a Russian agent. If his KGB masters got their hands on him, they would begin by interrogating him, and their methods would be the methods of the Beast. In short order Drummond would have told them everything of any conceivable value he had learned during his career with British Intelligence.

But that would not stop the torture. The agony would continue, and so would Drummond, babbling out anything that came to mind, making up stories from whole cloth, beyond response or understanding, wanting only that the torment be over.

It would be over only when Drummond was dead. But before that event, a hellish forever would pass.

Bolan could see the knowledge of Drummond's fate pass across the treasonous bastard's features.

"You are going to answer my questions," Bolan

told him, "and after that your friends—the friends you tried to betray—they take over. They promise not to turn you over. You get to spend the rest of your life in some cozy military prison, which is a hell of a lot more than you deserve."

"How civilized," Drummond murmured.

Bolan pushed the barrel of the Detonics into Drummond's high forehead, forcing his head back.

"At 11:35, an American-made Beechcraft C-12A Super King Air turboprop will land," the Englishman began tonelessly. "It has been converted for light cargo and bears Transworld Import/Export markings, although it is not one of MI5's. The pilot is Captain L. Rouballin of the KGB, and he will file a return flight plan for Leningrad."

"The prototype is here?"

Drummond nodded.

"Give me the envelope."

Drummond hesitated a moment, then pulled it out of his inside coat pocket. Reaching for it cost Bolan a serious spasm of pain in his left shoulder. He felt fresh stickiness on the wad of turtleneck that he was holding against the wound.

The envelope contained a single piece of 4-by-6-inch microfiche film. Bolan slipped it in the back pocket of his slacks, grimacing slightly as he did so.

Excellent. So far, so good. All that remained was to deal with the guidance-system prototype that the Russians were so hot for. As a piece of hardware it was not especially valuable; it was one of several which had been bread-boarded. It was the revealed technology that the Soviets wanted. The prototype sang openly of the secret history that had gone into its making. He would prevent this hemorrhage of data by keeping the thing out of their hands.

He would do this by giving it to them.

Of course, Bolan planned to make it a little bit too hot for them to handle.

5

Drummond was making it clear to the Russian that he did not appreciate being pressed into service as a stevedore. He had helped the KGBer load the prototype into the C-12A, but he was expressing his displeasure in no uncertain terms.

In the hangar office, Mack Bolan looked on grimly. The guy was good, all right, but then he had to be. He was playing for his life.

Bolan had showed him the face of his potential Executioner.

Agent Lemon still lay against the wall, unconscious but breathing regularly.

From the receiver on the desk in front of Bolan, Rouballin said, "Where is specifications manual?" The Russian pilot's voice was guttural and thick with a Slavic accent. There was a pause, and then Rouballin demanded, "What is meaning of this?" From the anger in his tone, Bolan knew Drummond had handed over the attaché case—the case that Bolan had been carrying.

"The manual is inside," Drummond's voice said suavely. "I will be most pleased to give you the combination to that lock—as soon as I am able to verify that the agreed-upon funds have been transferred to the account, in restitution for the advance I was compelled to make to the American, Mr. Charon.''

"You not get away with—"

"Of course, if you like you are free to break the case open," Drummond interrupted smoothly. "However, you should do so with a great deal of care. Do I make myself clear, old chap?"

The radio—another product of Gadgets Schwarz's fertile imagination and electronic wizardry—went silent for a moment; it was tuned to the frequency of a transmitting body-mike installed on Drummond

"If I were you, Captain Rouballin," the Brit went on, "I would consider my mission here accomplished. I suggest you get back in your craft and fly away home."

The KGB pilot muttered something in Russian that quickly faded to silent as he moved out of the microphone's range. Time passed, and then Bolan heard the sound of a PT6 engine turning over.

The bullet wound in his shoulder was a pulsing dull ache now. When Bolan peered under the improvised bandage, he found the redness looking angrier. But at least the bleeding was almost stopped. As he was re-covering it, Drummond came into the office.

There was a thin sheen of sweat across the double agent's forehead, but he had lost none of his composure. In a way, it was easier to deal with a professional like Drummond, who had enough years of tradecraft behind him to realize that his fate was dictated by his obedience now. From outside they heard the Beechcraft taxi by the hangar, the sound drifting into the distance, then coming back again, passing more quickly this time as the plane accelerated into take-off. Drummond listened to Bolan's instructions wordlessly.

Five minutes later Bolan had shed his bloody coat and the remnants of his turtleneck for the shirt and jacket of Lemon. It was a tight fit, but it would pass. The MI5 agent had regained consciousness, but some electrical wire and a rag from the hangar's maintenance shop insured his immobility and silence for now.

What was less sure, at least to the man who was engineering the play, was if he would last until the finale. The wound was a pounding presence now, and Bolan knew that without treatment he would descend into shock within minutes.

But there was still one more loose end to clean up before the mission would be history.

Shock would have to wait until then.

The control tower chief was a brisk efficient man in starched uniform shirtsleeves and forest-green slacks. He wore a mustache and full beard, both neatly trimmed, and a nameplate that identified him as "V. Vaughn." The tower rose from the midpoint of the three terminals, and through the panoramic windows Bolan could see 270 degrees worth of aprons and runways.

The tower chief glared at the camera case slung over Bolan's good shoulder and said, "No pictures," rather sharply. Then he frowned at the identification card in his hand for longer than necessary before handing it back to Sir Philip Drummond.

"What do you want?" Vaughn said, his tone barely civil.

"About twelve minutes ago," Drummond told the chief, "a Beechcraft manifested as belonging to Transworld I/E took off, bound for Leningrad. The aircraft ID number is SK4874. I would like to know that aircraft's present position."

Vaughn's frown deepened. "By regulation, Sir Philip, such a request must come through channels— as you know."

"Mr. Vaughn." Drummond raised his voice enough to turn the heads of a few of the air-traffic controllers working nearby. "This is an urgent matter, directly affecting national defense." He lowered his voice again. The guy had a flair for the dramatic, Bolan had to admit. But then, a man would have to become an accomplished actor if he expected to survive the double life.

"As tower chief," Drummond went on, "I believe you are aware of the functions of Transworld I/E?"

It was plain that Vaughn detested having rank pulled on him. But he spun on his heel and went to one of the vacant control terminals. He flicked a selector knob and a series of green-tinted images flashed onto the screen, each showing a different radar array. He studied one, then straightened.

"Approximate latitude 55 degrees, 50 minutes north," he announced. "Longitude 18 degrees, 32 minutes east. Heading roughly east-northeast."

Bolan was at the chart on the wall near the entry staircase. The KGB plane—and its cargo of top secret U.S. Navy defense equipment—was over the

Baltic Sea, and would be for about ten more minutes.

"If there is nothing else you require..." Vaughn began, in a tone that made it clear it hoped that were the case.

"A phone," Bolan said.

Vaughn looked at him for the first time. "Now, who might you—"

"Your office, Mr. Vaughn, if you please," Drummond broke in. "I assure you we will not be long."

The tower chief's office was a cubicle above the main control room, reached by a spiral staircase. To one side was a control terminal with a radio set to the control frequencies—for monitoring employee performance, Bolan guessed. Vaughn gave both men a suspicious glance, as if he were afraid they were going to steal something as soon as they were alone.

When he had gone, Bolan motioned Drummond into the chair. He unslung the camera case, lay it on Vaughn's desk, and let himself gingerly down beside it. Keeping his eye on his prisoner, Bolan allowed himself a moment of rest. The pain in his shoulder was becoming a presence, an increasing reminder that the beat had to be on double time now.

A panel on the camera case slid open to reveal a false bottom. Inside was an electric cord on a spring-loaded reel. Bolan pulled it out and plugged it in. Unclasping and lifting the lid revealed a simple control panel consisting of two toggle switches, a zero-center meter, a red indicator light, and a recessed button with a plastic safety cap.

This was another Gadgets Schwarz special, a radio transmitter designed to emit a low-power but extremely narrow beam of UHF impulse. It was adaptable to point-to-point communication, or as a remote control. It was now in the latter configuration.

Bolan flicked up the first toggle and a whip antenna extended from the case's top. He pointed it roughly east-northeast. When he worked the second toggle the meter's needle activated, veering to the left. Bolan corrected, and the needle trued toward center. The indicator light began to blink.

A few beats later it was a steady bright red, and the needle rode the zero-center mark.

In the attaché case aboard the KGB plane, which the pilot Rouballin believed contained the guidance systems spec manual, there was a homing device. The homing device was ganged to a remote detonator, which was in turn wired to about ten pounds of C-4 explosive. Now the homing device was sending a message back to its master.

Mack Bolan flipped the safety cap off the activator and sent a message back:

Greetings from the Man from Hellfire.

Bolan slumped where he sat, drained. His chest felt like someone was holding a red-hot branding iron against it, and he was aware his breathing had become ragged. The numbers were toppling down—right on him.

But the mission awaited confirmation.

He forced his fingers to accomplish the operation of repacking the remote detonator, then moved to Vaughn's radio monitor and turned it on. He clicked the channel selector, heard only routine communication until he hit the last frequency.

"Go ahead, TWA 1456," a controller in the room below said.

"Ah, Heathrow, we've got a possible situation here." The American pilot's voice had a faint Texas accent, cut by an obvious tension. He gave his coordinates, nearly the same ones Vaughn had announced for the Russian plane.

"Possible midair explosion," the pilot went on, "about ten miles off the port wing, five thousand feet lower. My copilot says he spotted a twin-engine just before it blew." There was an audible intake of breath, but when the pilot went on his voice was still studiously calm. "Ah, she just blew again, Heathrow, like the tanks just went. Please advise, Heathrow."

Bolan flicked the channel selector again. On another wavelength a woman controller's voice said, "Transworld I/E SK4874, please come in." She was repeating the call when Bolan turned the set off.

"It appears you have accomplished what you set out to," Drummond said without inflection.

Simply lifting his head to look at the other man had become a painful effort for Bolan.

Drummond smiled slightly and came fluidly out of the chair, lunged at Bolan, both arms outstretched.

Before his momentum could carry him across the desk, the Detonics was in Bolan's hand.

Drummond stopped himself short.

Bolan realized he had come damned close to firing. He was rapidly dropping below one hundred percent.

The other man realized it as well. "You haven't forgotten your ah, promise, have you?" Drummond inquired carefully.

Bolan shook his head. "You're the sellout, Drummond. Not me."

Drummond tried to reassemble the last shreds of his dignity. "Now then, there is no call—"

Bolan gestured with the little .45. "Let's get out of here," he said wearily.

6

"It was a screw-up, Colonel Phoenix," the American agent named Voorhis said. "A pure and simple screw-up."

"All right," Bolan said. He winced involuntarily as the sting of antiseptic bit into the wound in his shoulder.

The doctor was a slightly built youthful-looking man with bright red hair cut in an old-fashioned crew cut. He wore the insignia of a major in the regular British Army, Surgeon's Corps. The security-clearance card clipped to his breast pocket read "M. Goldstein, M.D."

Voorhis leaned against one white wall, watching the doctor work. "We contacted Whitehall," he went on. "We told them it was sensitive, that you'd have to go it alone after we collared Charon. They didn't like it, but they agreed."

Dr. Goldstein jabbed a hypodermic needle into the hard muscle of Bolan's thigh. "A synthetic antibiotic called Keflex," he informed his patient. "A precaution against blood infection."

"The bodyguard, Lemon, he'd been kept in the dark about Drummond, like most everyone," Voorhis said. "SOP for MI5, just like us. The one you're really keeping in the dark is the mole. But just before it went down, Whitehall was supposed to tip Lemon—and no one did. Damned sorry, Colonel.''

''Never mind,'' Bolan said blankly.

The agent mistook Bolan's tone. ''Listen, Colonel, there'll be a complete report. Heads will roll, depend on it.''

Bolan sighed. ''A complete report'' was the essence of every good bureaucracy. Why take direct action when you could dissect the problem from every angle in writing first? The only problem was that dissection never got you anywhere. But action sure as hell did.

In any case, there was no use dwelling on what was already irreversible. It was hardly the first time in all the years of warfare that Mack Bolan had been shot; it would likely not be the last. He would heal, and there would be other firefights to come.

The fighting man who tells you he has no belief whatsoever in luck is a liar. Mack Bolan was only thankful that so far in his good fight, little of his luck had been bad.

As for Lemon, the dedicated MI5 agent who risked his life to protect the man he believed to be his boss, Bolan held no rancor. In fact, his first inquiry had been about the guy, and he had been genuinely relieved to learn that the extent of Lemon's injuries was a bump on the head. Wittingly or unwittingly, Bolan had never done harm to a soldier of the same side.

''Charon?'' Bolan asked.

''He's here,'' Voorhis said quickly. ''I think he's going to cooperate.''

"I'll want to talk to him."

"I'll take care of it." Voorhis seemed happy at the chance to leave the room.

The doctor was taping gauze dressings over the two wounds. Cautiously, Bolan tried flexing the shoulder. It was possible, but it hurt.

"You will want to take it easy for some time, sir." The pain had not escaped Dr. Goldstein's notice. "I'm going to immobilize your left arm with a simple sling, to promote healing."

That would be okay, Bolan figured—at least until a new mission forced him to go hard again.

"Any bullet wound is serious," the doctor said, looping the sling over Bolan's right shoulder. "You were lucky, sir. Although both the trapezius and pec-. toral muscles are torn to some extent, there is no organ damage or bone fracture. As a unit, your left arm is entire and operative, but the muscle trauma will decrease your control over the arm and your general mobility as well."

The doctor rummaged in a cabinet, came out with a vial of pills. "This is oral Keflex. Take them until they are gone. I'll also prescribe some painkillers."

"No thanks." It had nothing to do with being stoic; Bolan could simply never afford to dull his senses with any drug.

"I see," the doctor said, in a tone that indicated he did not.

Bolan slid off the examining table and got his shirt—a spare one of his own—over his shoulders. "Thanks, Doc."

Dr. Goldstein flashed him a brisk salute.

Voorhis was waiting outside the infirmary. He led Bolan down a long white corridor, around a corner, and to an unmarked door. Bolan could hear the faint whirr of the ventilation that aired this underground London complex.

"Drummond?" Bolan said, palming the doorknob.

"Safe in the hands of MI5," Voorhis said. "At least safer than he'd be with his Russki pals."

Bolan nodded and went into the interrogation room.

Charon was composed, almost relaxed. He listened to what Bolan had to say, and offered neither objection nor defense. He seemed to view his defeat as simply another scientific phenomenon, a curiosity of life.

Of course he would cooperate, if it meant the possibility of leniency, he told Bolan. It would be illogical to do otherwise.

Outside in the corridor, Bolan found himself shaking with anger.

The bloodless detachment with which both Charon and Drummond seemed to view their treachery was awesome, and at the same time sad. The man who cannot understand treason, Bolan thought, neither can he understand patriotism. And the man without patriotism, without allegiance to the country of which he himself is an important part, is a lonely man indeed.

According to the technicality of law, neither man was guilty of a capital crime. According to Mack Bolan's worldview—a worldview forged in contemplation and tempered in terrorist blood—both men were as good as murderers. The mercenary sale of a military or intelligence secret in times of peace can have only one result:

To push a precariously balanced world that much closer to war and holocaust.

It was a direct subversion of a carefully created and mutually acceptable system of checks and balances, a subversion that could turn tension into violence. Bolan had learned again and again that too often the right weapon in the wrong hand added up to bloodshed.

It was the terrorists who pulled the triggers. But it was the Frederick Charons and the Sir Philip Drummonds of the world who put the guns in the jackals' hands.

Bolan got out a cigarette and lit a match onehanded. He hoped the smoke would clear the sour taste from his mouth.

Voorhis appeared at the corner of the hallway. "Communication from Washington, Colonel. Follow me, please."

The room into which Voorhis led him contained a wooden desk with a chair and nothing else. In the exact center of the desk was a telephone. Voorhis nodded in its direction and went out, shutting the door behind him.

Bolan picked up the handset. For several seconds there was a hash of electronic squeals and bursts of static, indicating that a scrambler was interfacing with the line. Then a deep familiar voice said, "Striker."

"Go ahead, Hal."

The satellite-transmitted voice of head fed Harold Brognola was thin and tinny, but the anxiety in its tone came through five-by. "What happened?"

"You've already checked that out, Hal," Bolan said patiently.

"Sure. An accident, they said."

"That's what it was. It happens that way in real life sometimes, Hal, no matter how clean you lay it out. I'll be all right. Give it time."

"Sure, Striker," Brognola said quickly. "With Frederick Donald Charon and Sir Philip Drummond neutralized, you're on R and R as of right now."

Brognola paused, and the static rose up to fill the silence. But the message in Brognola's tone was as clear as if he had gone on talking.

Mack Bolan had not lived this long by betting his life on other men, unless he felt he knew them damned well. But he had bet his life on Hal Brognola more than once, because that man he knew like his own brother.

Right now, that knowledge told the wounded warrior what Brognola had not:

Time had just run out. R and R was bullshit.

"Something has broken, hasn't it, Hal?"

"What about Charon?" Brognola asked, evading the question.

"He's agreed to talk. The computer boys are debriefing him right now. Aaron should have everything he needs to tap into the DonCo mainframe. The station here will send via scrambled telex within the hour."

"Aaron is standing by," Brognola said. "And he ought to be able to find enough bloody fingerprints in Charon's data banks to put the guy on ice for a long time. That's one leak plugged." Brognola sighed. "And two more are probably springing open as we're talking."

"We'll plug them as we find them, Hal," Bolan replied evenly. This man who had pledged his being to the good fight had long ago accepted the basic facts of life. Sure, the terrorist campaigns comprised a war of containment, a constant battle to beat down the brush fires of armed aggression whenever and wherever they flared. But it was spontaneous combustion, and it would go on forever, or until men no longer tried to dominate other men through intimidation, repression, terror. It was war everlasting, war that might never be won.

But Bolan knew it was worth the fight.

"Something else has broken, Hal," Bolan repeated. "I want to know what it is."

Static crackled again, long enough to allow Bolan to get a cigarette lit. This hesitation was characteristic of the Justice Department Fed. Hal Brognola was no by-the-book bureaucrat by any means, but a lifetime in government service molds a man, for sure, and he had never been entirely comfortable with Mack Bolan's free-lance status. As early as the Miami blitz against the Cosa Nostra, Brognola had extended a clandestine olive branch, what amounted to an official hunting license—with the condition that the Executioner answer to, and take orders from, Justice. Bolan had refused. He wanted no sanction; in fact, he plainly acknowledged that by every rule of society he was an outlaw. The cop in Hal Brognola knew this as well.

But the patriot in him knew that Bolan was getting results. The Mafia was falling over like so many ducks in a carnival shooting gallery, and the nation Brognola was sworn to protect was growing stronger daily for the Executioner's efforts.

In the end, Brognola and Bolan struck a compromise. The new war against terrorism was too broad, too awesome, and too great a threat to the future of this globe. No one man could take it on alone—but if one man existed who could spearhead the campaign, that man was Mack Bolan. When the complete backing of the Sensitive Operations Group of the Department of Justice were offered, Bolan accepted.

With conditions.

The Stony Man Farm command complex, nestled in the shadow of Virginia's Blue Ridge Mountains, was Bolan's domain. The Stony Man team—April Rose, Aaron Kurtzman, Able Team, Phoenix Force, and all the rest of them—were his people, personally handpicked, answerable to no one but him. Bolan would operate as he always had.

With responsibility. And with direct and effective action.

Yeah, effective it had been. From the jungles of Panama and the high-mountain country of eastern Turkey, to the Algerian desert and beyond, the terrorist cadres had gotten a taste of something the Mafia had grown to know—and hate.

It was called the Bolan Effect. And it worked.

Hal Brognola thanked God that it was working for their side. If all Bolan required in exchange was a free hand, he'd damn well have it.

"What do you remember about Frank Edwards?" Brognola said.

Edwards had been a back-burner project of the Stony Team for some time, and Bolan was familiar with the broad outlines of the man's dossier.

"Ex-CIA," Bolan said. "Suspected of freelancing for various Arab radical factions in the Middle East. He's also been fingered as having worked in an advisory capacity for Amin in Uganda and Khaddafi in Libya, training and tradecraft, if I remember correctly."

"You do, Striker," Brognola confirmed. "Add to that gunrunning—we believe he's been acting as the middleman in the illegal shipment of American armament ultimately destined for terrorist hands. But he's beyond our official reach, and even if he weren't, we couldn't put him on trial, because we'd have to make top-secret intelligence public in order to present the evidence against him."

"But we would like to see him take a fall."

"He's *got* to take a fall, Striker," Brognola said. "New intelligence has just come in on the guy, and if I read it right, he's got his finger in a far bigger pie than we ever suspected. Not only that, but it ties in with Charon. Edwards has to be interdicted, and now."

Bolan ground out his cigarette butt on the concrete floor of the barren underground room. "Take it from the top, Hal."

"Right. We're telexing you Edwards's updated dossier and a data package, but here's the bare bones of it. Edwards's personal staff, the half dozen or so he employs for security, communications, liaison with his terrorist clients, and other 'housekeeping' duties, are all Americans. They're either ex-Special Forces, or ex-Agency, like him."

Like him, for sure. Another nest of treasonous vipers, men in whose lexicon words like "loyalty" and "patriotism" had been replaced by "power-lust" and "self-interest." Yeah, Edwards needed to take a fall, and Bolan would be more than happy to give him the push.

"More than six months ago, we infiltrated one of our people into Edwards's organization. Because Edwards is a highly trained operative himself and still maintains a vast network of clandestine contacts within the international intelligence community, we had to make it look absolutely authentic. Only three people knew the truth: the agent, myself, and the commander in chief. That'll give you an idea how badly we want Edwards.

"Following orders, the agent sold some factual but outdated information to a KGB counterintel operator, was caught, and was cashiered of course. As far as the agency knows—and her files support this—she was drummed out after a long and valued career because she turned rotten. Even her closest colleagues believe it. It had to be that way, because we believe it's possible that Edwards may even have a pipeline into the agency. It worked. Within a week the approach to Edwards was made, and within a month she was in."

Bolan had not missed the feminine pronoun. An idea started to take shape in his mind—and he did not like the look of it.

"This was projected as a long-term operation, to be conducted with absolute minimum risk of error. For that reason, our agent has contacted us exactly twice in those six months. In the first instance, she informed us that Edwards was just as professional as we believed. He was treating her as what she was: a highly trained and proficient operative. No grab-ass bullshit or anything like that. She had been given a few assignments, nothing very sensitive—courier duty, surveillance, intelligence analysis, and so forth. Edwards was testing her out, and she was passing with flying colors. He was convinced that she was what she professed to be: a fellow professional—and a fellow traitor."

"Hal," Bolan interrupted. "Who is she?"

"You know her, Striker. The name is Toby Ranger."

Bolan leaned back in the straight-backed wooden chair and let out breath.

Yeah, he knew Toby Ranger.

In that other lifetime, when the Mafia menace took him the length and breadth of the country, fate had engineered the intersection of his path with that of Toby Ranger more than once. He had fought at the woman's side. He had saved her life.

And she had saved his.

So maybe "know" wasn't quite the right word. Maybe it would be more accurate to say that the lives of Mack Bolan and Toby Ranger were bonded, in a way few men and women could ever hope to know.

"Striker, listen—" Hal began.

"You said Toby made two contacts," Bolan broke in, his voice betraying no emotion. "Brief me on the second."

"It's fresh, Striker—came in while you were airborne en route to Heathrow. Last week, Edwards held some kind of big meet at a chalet he owns in the Swiss Alps, in the canton of Valais. Nominally, Edwards now holds Swiss citizenship. Anyway, this chalet is apparently one of his permanent bases. He maintains a full-time security force there, multinational, recruited from the terrorists he serves—as opposed to his handpicked inner-circle force that Toby became a part of. The chalet also has a communications facility. Probably Edwards has other bases like it, but he's never domiciled in one place for long.

"As near as Toby could make out, something damned big was being hatched at this meet. Those people weren't terrorists, at least not what we usually think of as terrorists. Toby was pretty sure they were intelligence agents, representing nearly every free-world nation. Some of them were 'retired' like Edwards, but some of them were still active, we think. Besides the agents, there were a few others offering 'specialized services.' One of them was Frederick Charon."

Brognola's voice had gone harsh with tension and suppressed rage. "Do you have any guesses as to what this could mean, Striker?"

"An international underground intelligence network," Bolan said evenly. "A 'black' CIA, run by men trained by the top legit agencies in the world, serving the needs of the terrorist network. With state-of-the-art technology provided by traitors like Charon.''

"That's the way it shapes up," Brognola agreed. "And it has to be stopped."

So the mission wasn't over after all; in fact, it had hardly begun. The Charon penetration, the cutting of the Charon-Drummond-KGB chain, was only a foot in the door of a major infrastructure of deceit, treason, and terror. Somewhere in the bowels of that infrastructure sat Frank Edwards, renegade agent, death merchant.

And it was up to Mack Bolan to bring that temple of terror crashing down on him, burying him forever.

"Where is Edwards, Hal?"

"Striker, you're in no shape to take him on, not now. That bullet wound—"

"Where is he?"

Brognola's sigh cut through the static. "We don't know."

Bolan waited. The idea in his mind was getting uglier.

"Toby was only able to pass what I've told you. She was leaving the Valais chalet, but she wasn't sure for where." Another pause. "I'll level, Striker. She suspects her cover might be blown."

The ugly idea was clear as a photograph now. Frank Edwards operated in a grim dark world, and the realities of that world were overwhelmingly lethal.

Toby Ranger would remain among the living only until she had revealed everything she knew to Frank

Edwards. And Edwards and his men would know every vicious method for encouraging her to talk.

The odds that Toby was alive were short. The odds that she was entire were almost nil.

"We're not even sure where the Valais chalet is located, Striker," Brognola said bleakly.

The phone handset cradled against his shoulder, Bolan was using his right hand to undo the sling. The pain was down to a dull ache, and the arm itself would serve—if he could control it.

"I know how to find out," Bolan said grimly.

"Striker?"

"What?"

Brognola started to say something, seemed to change his mind. "Live large," he murmured, and Bolan heard the connection break.

The sound of the chair legs on the floor seemed unnaturally loud in the bare room, and the door creaked when Bolan went out.

It was time for one last conversation with Frederick Charon.

7

The dark-haired guy was trying to blink cigarette smoke out of his eyes and bring around the M-16 carbine at the same time. He had accomplished neither when the silenced 9mm slug tore through his throat.

The cigarette dropped from his lips as he went down, and blood geysered from the jagged wound to stain the grass on which he fell. Then, almost lazily on the clean twilight mountain air, smoke drifted from the same gory hole, as the guy's lungs rejected the inhalation that was his last living act.

Mack Bolan grabbed the guy, who had been dying for a smoke, by his heels and dragged him under the canopy of the lower branches of one of the stunted larches that dotted the steep slope, before melting into the shadows of the trees himself. The exertion cost him some pain from the tightly bandaged shoulder, but he needed time for surveillance before moving in. The encounter with the guard had been chance, but it did not mean the numbers were up yet. It could be some time before the guy was missed.

Right now time was not Mack Bolan's ally.

His chronometer, now set to Switzerland local time, read 2010; within a few minutes it would be full dark. He had left London less than five hours before, in a Lear-jet nominally registered to a British citizen, but flown by a crackerjack RAF pilot. At Cointrin Airport in Geneva a chopper was waiting to transport him to Sion on the Rhone River, capital of the Alpine canton of Valais. A Land Rover loaded with the equipment Colonel John Phoenix had requisitioned awaited him.

It was undoubtedly some of the most beautiful country in the world, with its crystal-clear mountain streams bisecting the rugged scarps of the towering peaks. Driving west, Bolan passed through groves of larch trees and hornbeam; a marmot darted across the road. But the thought of the traitor Frank Edwards—and the woman who was likely now his prisoner—occupied Bolan and allowed him only the most superficial appreciation of the extraordinary terrain.

At Sierre he turned the Rover south, up the Anniviers Valley. He passed the power station at Vissoie, the tiny resort towns of Ayer and Zinal. Soon after that, about thirty miles after he left the Rhone Valley, the gravel road narrowed, and less than two miles further on a posted gate announced that it was a private access from that point on. Rigging for combat, Bolan went EVA.

Ten minutes of dogtrotting had brought him to his present position—and to the guard who had just learned that like the pack said, smoking *was* hazardous to your health.

Due south Bolan could see the Matterhorn, marking the border with Italy, and off to the west the Dufourspitze, at 15,200 feet the highest peak in

Switzerland. The glaciers that never melted streaked the sides of the rugged Pennine Alpine range.

The dusk that had already pervaded the steep-walled valley for hours began to rapidly purple now, but it would be a cloudless starry night. That suited Bolan's purpose perfectly.

From a pocket of his military web belt he removed a Litton Miniature Night Vision Pocket Scope, the compact NVD no bigger than the palm of his hand. Designated the M-841, the second-generation image intensifier used passive low light operation; that is, it amplified available light, no matter how dim, five hundred times, focusing it on a viewing screen. An automatic brightness control counteracted blooming, and the second-generation microchannel plate completely eliminated streaking of the image.

From another pouch Bolan selected the objective lens, an eight-step zoom whose magnification ranged from seven-tenths of unity to 4X, at f-stops from 1.8 to 22. Screw mounted to the pocket scope, it formed a unit about five inches long, weighing under two pounds.

The chalet where Edwards had recently called his "black" CIA organizational meeting, and which he maintained as one of several permanent bases, sat about one hundred meters from and twenty above Bolan's surveillance position. The building rose three stories, each story encircled with an ornate balcony fashioned in a Bavarian style; the peaked roof was baroque with gingerbread trim, and topped by a weathercock. It could have been any one of the hundreds of small resorts that dotted this Alpine high country.

Instead it was an operations center for a brilliantly twisted one-time U.S. agent now turned terrorist mercenary.

Alpine meadow surrounded the place out to the perimeter where Bolan had taken his position; a drive of crushed gravel curved up to the entrance—a canopied parking apron like the entrance to a hotel, which is what the building had likely been at one time. Bolan focused the NVD in that direction, clicked up to 2.4X magnification, and picked out three 4WD rigs and a Toyota longbed pickup truck.

Bolan had made three other guards in addition to the dead man under the larch. Similarly armed with M-16s, they were walking the perimeter, and not paying a hell of a lot of attention to their work. That was going to turn out to be a deadly mistake.

These men did not project the alertness or polish of well-trained operatives. Bolan figured they were the terrorist gang-members on loan to Edwards for routine security.

Except the Executioner was about to break up the routine.

Above the canopy fronting the chalet, light flashed as a door to the balcony opened and shut. Bolan zoomed the Litton to full 4X magnification, and picked out the man, standing with both hands on the railing, scanning the dark grounds. He was about forty, in wire-rimmed glasses and modishly long hair, and he wore a nylon windbreaker against the chill of the spring mountain air.

Among the data package that Stony Man Farm had telexed to London were five photographs, which Bolan had committed to his eidetic memory. The faces in the photos, of four men and one woman, were of American Intelligence agents who had severed their official relationship with their agency within the prior six months under any circumstances which could be considered unusual.

One of the faces belonged to the man on the balcony. His name was Corey James, and he had been with the CIA for fourteen years, including two when he was posted to Western European Section, then headed by one Frank Edwards. His file had been closed with the notation: "Voluntary retired, highest service rating."

That would have to be replaced by: "Turncoat."

Bolan guessed that if a man of James's caliber were on-site, it would be as chief of operations at the chalet. As such he would be able to tell Bolan quite a bit.

Whether he wished to or not.

Bolan came out of his crouch. It was time to go hard.

On Bolan's right wrist was what looked like a thick metallic bracelet with a one-inch length of wooden dowling attached. Bolan nestled the dowel between the second and third fingers of his right hand and pulled, and the head end of a two-and-a-half-foot length of spring-loaded piano wire unreeled from inside the bracelet, like the starter on a lawn mower.

But it was immediately and painfully apparent to

Bolan that there was no way the torn shoulder muscle would allow him to raise his left arm high enough to put the garrote to deadly use. It was not a situation he was pleased with, but the reminder of his limitation was useful. Mack Bolan was no wild-ass warrior with a knife between his teeth and a blazing gun in each hand, charging heedlessly into a hail of lead. He was realistically aware of his mortality and his capabilities. Right now those capabilities were limited in a way he wasn't used to. But that would only change his methods, not his effectiveness—as long as he kept in mind the restriction the wound was imposing.

Bolan let the spring tension recoil, and reached for the sheath on his left hip.

The second guard only managed to get out half of a gurgling cry as the Fairbairon-Sykes commando stiletto sliced through the flesh of his neck to sever the jugular vein, but one of his buddies was near enough to hear it. The bodycock called out, "Ahmed," softly, and followed it with a guttural string of Arabic ending in a questioning intonation. As Bolan let the dead-weight of Ahmed drop to the ground, the shape of the other guard came into view.

The guy must have spotted Bolan at the same time.

He tried to bring up his M-16 while twisting to make himself a smaller target, and the mistake of thinking defense when he should have been thinking offense gave Bolan the millisecond he needed. The guard was still lining out his shot when a 9mm skull-buster cored into his temple and on through into the night, a spray of red and gray its wake.

Ninety seconds later, darkness covered the blitzer's

path as he eased below the canopy fronting the chalet. Behind him, the same darkness hid the body of the fourth guard, heavier by the weight of three silenced 9mm slugs.

Because neither the time frame nor the chalet's physical layout allowed for a full-cover preliminary softprobe, the nightfighter had rigged up for every contingency up to an all-out firefight. His guess was that there were fewer than four bodycocks inside, the relief crew for the men now littering the lawn, plus Corey James and his technical support people. But if the chalet's forces went beyond that, Bolan was ready.

He wore the skintight blacksuit that had been specially designed of a rip-stop elasticized material by the same NASA scientists who outfitted the astronauts. The suit served another purpose beyond its obvious value as camouflage: it gave its wearer a significant psychological edge. The sight of the big black apparition, weapons dangling from shoulder and hip, had startled more than one enemy into momentary hesitation—which abruptly ended along with the enemy's life.

A military canvas web belt hugged the waist of the outfit, the hook-and-eye flat bronze buckle snapping fast. The Fairbairon knife rode the left hip, and the Executioner's newest side arm rode the right.

Stony Man armorer Konzaki had introduced Bolan to the recently developed Beretta Model 93R. The production model was a true machine pistol, which meant it could be fired on full automatic with one hand. For improved accuracy and control, however, it was fitted with a fold-down front handle and an elongated trigger guard; the fingers of the left hand wrapped around the handle, and the guard accommodated the thumb. The side-by-side magazine held fifteen steel-jacketed 9mm cartridges; a sixteenth nestled in the chamber.

Konzaki had modified to Bolan's specifications the 93R he was now carrying. With the installation of a suppressor and specially machined springs designed to cycle subsonic cartridges, the Beretta was effectively silenced. A selector switch offered the options of single-shot fire or three-round bursts, at a reduced cyclic rate of 110 rounds per minute. The result was extraordinary auto-fire accuracy, particularly in the hands of a marksman like Mack Bolan. For gun-leather, Konzaki had customized an oversized one-piece holster with a plasticized friction-reduction lining that reduced to almost zero the possibility of hang-up by the gun's sights or hammer.

Bolan's submachine gun was the new Israeli Uzi. Konzaki had fitted it with a flash-hider, and it was throated to feed 9mm Parabellum hollow-points. The armorer had also welded two 32-cartridge magazines together at a right angle, so that when Bolan inserted one into the magazine well of the pistol grip, the other extended forward parallel to the barrel. Not only did this facilitate speed-loading, but the extra front-end weight helped compensate against barrel-climb during auto-fire. The Uzi's change lever was all the way forward in the A (auto) position.

In addition to the web belt's pouches, Bolan wore a military hip pack with a capacity of nearly a half cubic foot. He would have preferred the size and comfort of a backpack, but there was no point in additionally straining his torn shoulder.

Bolan used the Litton M-841 for a quickscan of his backtrack, saw no sign that there had been more than the four guards. He stowed the NVD and moved on to the chalet's door.

From there on in, the play would have to be by the ear.

Beyond the front doors, the first floor was still laid out like the hotel lobby it had once been. Several chairs and two sofas were arranged before a fireplace, and the front desk was off to one side. Beyond the desk was a staircase.

A swarthy guy in fatigues with no insignia was sitting in one of the chairs, facing the doors. There was an M-16 in his lap, and on top of it a girlie magazine opened to the centerfold. The guy's head was back, and his eyes were closed.

Through the crack where the doors met, Bolan could see a thrown deadbolt.

He set the silenced Beretta on single-shot and put a slug into the bolt.

The impact didn't make much noise, but it was enough to wake the door guard. He shook sleep out of his eyes, threw the magazine across to the sofa, and got cautiously up, the auto-carbine at port arms. Bolan saw he was also wearing a military .45 automatic pistol in a holster.

When he was close enough to see the busted lock, Bolan came through the door.

Then the guy was pinned hard against the wall, the

M-16 immobilized by the press of Bolan's body, a handful of his blouse twisted into Bolan's hard fist, which pressed into his chest. The wall was covered with flowered paper, beginning to fade.

Bolan let the guy have a very close look at the end of the Beretta's suppressor. "Where's Corey James?"

The guy opened his mouth to gasp in air, but it was a lousy attempt at a stall. Bolan anticipated the move before the guy had started it, letting go of the pinned M-16 and clawing for the .45 on his hip.

The Beretta made a soft *pffutt* and spit a 9mm whizzer into the guy's face. Stuff came out of the back of his head and dripped down over the faded flowers.

Bolan's sensitive hearing picked up footsteps on the staircase.

The first guy followed instinct and tried to get in the opening shot, and took a three-round burst from navel to neck for his trouble. The second guy followed common sense, and faced the blacksuited nightfighter with both hands over his head.

Bolan used the barrel of the Beretta to motion the guard down the rest of the stairs, then back against the wall next to the fireplace. He was a big-boned black man, and the gaze he gave Bolan was sullen. But then he saw the nearly headless corpse sprawled on the other side of the room, and his eyes widened in fear.

"James," Bolan said, crossing to him, the Beretta big in his fist. He stopped three feet from the black man, did not touch him. "Where is he?"

The black pointed with his chin. "Downstairs. Only one door there." He spoke with a thick West Indian accent. "You gonna kill me too?"

"You're already dead, guy," Bolan said. He laid the suppressor against the black's temple, his hand moving fast as thought, and the guy went down like a sledgehammered cow. Blood glistened along his hair-line.

No sound came from the chalet's bowels.

Bolan did not like leaving the bodies there in the open, even for a few minutes. But there was greater risk in not reconning.

He did not want his upcoming chat with Corey James to be interrupted.

The second and third floors were occupied by rooms bisected by a single long corridor. Light shone under the door of one on the second floor, but when Bolan kicked into it he found it empty, although it was clearly someone's quarters. The name on an old envelope identified the someone as Corey James.

If the lobby and the upper floors had been left as they were when the place was a hotel, the basement had undergone some remodelling, for sure. Bolan cat-footed down carpeted stairs. At the bottom there was a short entryway passage that jogged hard right after a few steps. At its corner a video camera on a motor mount was sweeping the entryway.

Bolan put a slug into the lens.

Beyond the corner the featureless hallway ended ten feet farther on in a windowless door. The door swung open and an M-16-armed gunman came charging out.

He charged into a three-round swarm of 9mm stingers that stopped him cold.

Behind the fresh corpse the door started to swing shut. Bolan's right shoulder hit it before the motion could be completed, and the door swung wide again. Someone grunted with pain and crashed into something.

Corey James turned and looked at the black-clad intruder without expression. Over shirtsleeves he wore an automatic in a shoulder holster, but he made no move toward it.

The efforts toward maintaining the chalet's original Old World elegance had been foregone down here in favor of modern expediency. The basement consisted of a single large windowless room, and it was obviously the nerve center of Edwards's Alpine base. One wall was lined with a control panel fronted by swivel chairs. There were keyboard terminals, video display tubes, two computer-tape transports, several radio transceivers and a couple of telephones. And it looked like the guy was still in the process of outfitting the place. Along the adjacent wall were stacked a couple dozen crates of various sizes, most of them stenciled, "Fragile—Electronic Components—Avoid Extreme Heat or Cold."

Corey James was standing at the console, next to a man who was seated in one of the swivel chairs. Another technician lay behind the door that Bolan had slammed into him; a goulash of electronic parts was scattered on the floor around him. The guy was trying to shake off his daze, but he didn't look hurt.

Bolan wished he could say the same. The body

blow he had taken coming in, even though he had tried to absorb it on his good side, had cost him more than pain. He thought he had felt the traumatized muscle tear a bit, and there was a warm wetness under the dressing on the left side of his chest. As he straightened, a sharp pinch of hurt darted across it.

The traitorous ex-CIA agent across the room coolly regarding him would have been enough to arouse Bolan's righteous anger. The wound enhanced it.

"They're dead, James," he snapped. "Your amateur bodyguards weren't good enough. You ought to do something about security."

James nodded toward the crates. "You were a week early."

"Too bad."

Bolan holstered the Beretta; the necessity for silence was past. He held the Uzi by the pistol grip, letting the lanyard support its weight.

Yeah, one more week. One week, and this base would have been in full operation, with capacity as a safehouse, communications center, data-retrieval facility. Not even a headquarters, but only one of many bases just like it, the foundation of a scheme unlike any Bolan had encountered in all the days of the New Terrorist Wars.

Bolan had long been aware that most of the terrorist organizations were loosely linked in an informal network. But for the most part the ideological hate-mongers were poorly trained at best, under-financed and -armed, and too suspicious and jealous to fully trust their so-called allies.

But Frank Edwards, and the people like Corey

James to whom he had chosen to delegate responsibility, were experts, trained in the black arts by the finest intelligence outfits on the globe, the training backed by years of experience. Their contacts in the shadow world of international intrigue were vast, and by dint of their one-time official sanction, they had access to the most advanced technology in the free world. Not only that, but Edwards apparently had the money to pay for it. But that was no surprise; illicit arms smuggling could be immensely profitable, with terrorists desperate for firepower willing to pay markups of several hundred percent. As a business, it was hard to beat.

If you didn't mind trading in death.

Now Edwards, along with other renegade agents of his ilk, were consolidating their resources to form a private intelligence agency. International in scope, wide-reaching in capacity, staffed by experienced men who still retained entree into most corners of the worldwide underground, it would rival the official bureaus of many free nations.

And it would service those sworn to turn free nations into slave states.

Mack Bolan was determined to see that would not happen. He owed it to the world—and to one brave woman named Toby Ranger.

"Where's Edwards?" Bolan asked, his voice steel-cold.

"I don't know," James said calmly.

The guy knew all the tricks, and he tried one now. With his right hand he adjusted his wire-rimmed glasses, let the hand linger there. He held out his left,

gestured with it vacantly, a protestation of inno-
cence—and a polished piece of misdirection of attention.

The hand at the glasses shot across the twelve
inches that separated it from the shoulder holster, got
fingers around gun butt.

It was a good trick, sure. But Bolan had seen it
before.

The Uzi stuttered a four-shot burst into the smart
guy's outstretched left hand.

The report was an eardrum-straining crack in the
enclosed room, and it brought a ragged croak of pain
from Corey James. The hollow-point 9mm flesh-
shredders had left nothing at the end of his left arm
but a mangled stump of bone and gore.

The dazed technician on the floor turned deathly
pale and lurched onto his hands and knees, whatever
he'd had for supper spewing out of his mouth and
nostrils. As Bolan had figured, before putting in with
the turncoat network, the guy had been a desk
jockey; the "wet" side of intelligence work was new
to him. The other technician was a little cooler. He
shucked his lab coat and went to James.

The ex-agent was ghostly white himself, halfway
into shock already. He sunk into one of the swivel
chairs. The technician tore a long strip from his coat,
wrapped the rest around the shreds of blood-soaked
flesh that had been James's hand. With the reserved
strip he began to fashion a tourniquet around
James's forearm. There was fear in the glance he
gave the Uzi when Bolan poked James with its snout,
but he continued his work.

"Where is Frank Edwards?" Bolan said, each word deliberate as a death knell.

The guy looked up at him, and Bolan could read the knowledge in his eyes.

James was seeing a vision of his own death, and he knew that vision was a heartbeat from becoming reality.

"I'm not sure," James muttered, teeth clenched against the pain.

Bolan prodded him with the submachine gun. "When you stop talking, you stop living."

"Edwards left yesterday evening. A while back, he took an apartment in Rome, rigged it up as a safe-house, a place where he could go to ground if he had to. He'd done some work for the Red Brigades—the Italian terrorist group—and some of their people housekeep, in exchange for using the place. That's where Frank said he was going."

James's face was drawn with pain. "I don't know if he was leveling with me, and if he was, why he was going there. My guess is he was just trying to leave a hard-to-follow trail. He might be there. He might not. But that's all I can tell you." James's longish hair was damp with the sweat of hurt and fear. "That's the truth. Your killing me won't make it less true."

"What about the woman?"

"Ranger? She left with him."

"Was she all right?"

"Sure. Why wouldn't she. . . ." Faint light cut the pain in James's eyes. He tried for a smile that came out a grimace instead. "So she *was* one of yours.

Frank had an idea about that. Maybe that's why he headed for Rome. Those Red Brigades people specialize in kidnapping for ransom. They know a little about coercion.''

"Where is the Rome place?"

James's skin was the color of chalk, and his eyes were starting to glaze. Bolan jabbed the barrel of the Uzi into his chest, hard enough to hurt.

"Okay, okay." James's voice was weak and reedy, but he managed to mutter an address. He just got it out before his chin fell forward to his chest, and his eyes turned glassy.

"Get him away from there," Bolan told the technicians. The guy on the floor got shakily to his feet. The front of his lab coat was stained with his own vomit.

It took only seconds for Bolan to dig the goop from the hip pack, mold it to the console in a few strategic spots, and set sixty-second fuses. The two technicians recognized plastique, all right; Bolan had no trouble getting them to hoist James and drag him up the stairs and out of the chalet.

There were five-gallon jerricans of gasoline strapped to the backs of each of the 4WD rigs parked out front, which made things easier. Bolan uncapped them, splashed their contents over the inside of the three vehicles as well as the cab of the Toyota pickup.

From the bowels of the chalet there was a dull boom. By the time Bolan had finished emptying the gas cans, he could see flames licking up the stairway into the chalet's lobby.

James and the two technicians backed away down the slope. But Bolan had lost interest in them.

He selected an HE grenade from a belt pouch, pulled the pin, and rolled it into the back of the nearest 4WD, then dogtrotted down the slope.

Behind him the grenade's explosion shattered the night. A moment later the vehicles' gas tanks began to blow, like a string of gigantic firecrackers.

Bolan paused at the tree-line perimeter. A huge ball of gasoline-fed fire was eating into the canopy, moving to meet the flame now consuming the chalet's first floor. Windows began to implode. As Bolan watched, the canopy creaked and collapsed, tearing framing from the building's facade.

James and the technicians stood halfway down the slope, looking small and helpless in the fire's hellish glow.

One small part of Frank Edwards's "black" CIA was destroyed, but the guy himself was still at large, somewhere.

And somewhere a woman's life hung by a thread— a thread tied to that same Frank Edwards.

It had been on the heartbeat. Now it was in the hands of fate.

8

The street was called the Via del Gladiatori, the Way of the Gladiator. It was an appropriate reminder to Mack Bolan of the cosmic scheme, and his own small role in it.

Today, most people saw the ancient gladiator of this city of Rome as a figure of courage and romance. In fact, he was neither. True, a few did choose to step into the bloody arena of the Roman Colosseum of their own free will; one was the second-century Roman emperor, Commodus. But most gladiators were slaves or criminals, forced to fight on threat of death. There was no romance to it at all, and whatever courage the gladiator brought to his combat was generated through the will to survive.

Few did. In victory, the gladiator won only the right to fight again. Defeat was usually synonymous with death. In the rare case in which the losing gladiator survived the combat, his fate was given over to the paying spectators. If they waved their handkerchiefs, he was given clemency; if they turned down their thumbs, he was executed.

In the long sordid history of mankind, few spectacles rivaled the gladiatorial combat before tens of thousands of bloodthirsty citizens for the sheer savagery of which Animal Man was capable.

Now Mack Bolan stood against another manifestation of that savagery, the bestiality of international terrorism. Its perpetrators existed outside of law, society, or civilization. Though they sometimes carried on about "liberation," "power to the people," and "democratic revolution," their creed was control, suffocation, and the eradication of anyone standing in their way.

The Red Brigades, the "housekeepers" of Frank Edwards's Rome safe-apartment, were a prime example. The best known of the groups that made up the loose-knit Italian terrorist coalition known as The Organization, the Brigades depicted themselves as noble crusaders for freedom and human rights. However, one way they chose to demonstrate this high-minded commitment was with the kidnapping of statesman Aldo Moro, leader of the Italian Christian Democratic Party, in 1978. Five of Moro's bodyguards were ruthlessly cut down in a barrage of gunfire. Fifty-five days later, Moro himself was found— in the trunk of a car, his body riddled with bullets.

If undeterred, the terrorists would replace freedom with repression, tolerance with persecution, initiative with intimidation, independence with enslavement. Their principal weapon was mindless violence. They recognized no order except anarchy and chaos. The world they wanted to build would be created for them alone.

That was why Mack Bolan had chosen to stand between them and that damnable goal.

The tireless warrior was no gladiator. He had not been forced into this fight but had chosen it of his own free will. Nor was he kin to those ancient blood-lustful Romans who had crowded the stadiums to see the sands flow red; he took no pleasure in battle for its own sake, had no deranged need to wash his hands in his enemies' gore.

It was far more simple than that. Mack Bolan knew that passive lip service to the desirability of a better world would never be enough. As the statesman Edmund Burke had written, "The only thing necessary for the triumph of evil is for good men to do nothing."

It was as elemental as that. And Mack Bolan could no more do nothing than stop breathing.

He did not know how the long war would end, but of one thing he was certain: it would not end in surrender.

The only ultimate failure was the failure to act.

Sometimes a man had to be willing to die for what was right.

And sometimes a man had to be willing to kill.

When Bolan had removed the dressing that Dr. Goldstein had applied to the bullet wound, it was spotted with fresh blood. Now the pain was a constant presence. He pushed it to the back of his mind and concentrated on the building across the Via del Gladiatori.

It was a modern nondescript cube, a six-story apartment building, not fancy but probably far from cheap, especially in this city where housing was perpetually at a premium. Balconies hung from the front

and the right side; their arrangement indicated there
were four apartments to a floor.

It was around midnight, and traffic was light. The
Via del Gladiatori was part of the belt highway that
ringed Rome about six miles out from its center; this
district was called the Esposizione Universale di
Roma. A block north, the glass face of a slablike sky-
scraper rose to dominate the area; it was the headquarters of an international corporation. Behind it
flowed the Tiber River, and on the other side Bolan
could make out the dome of the covered stadium that
had been built for the 1960 Olympic Games.

Movement caught Bolan's eye.

The apartment he had been watching was on the
fourth floor, toward the back. Light shone faintly
beyond drawn curtains faced by a sliding glass door
and opening on the balcony. Someone was moving
through it.

Bolan set the zoom lens of the Litton Night Vision
Pocket Scope to full 4X, and the upper half of a
woman's figure swam into view. For a moment he
felt a tightness across his chest that had nothing to do
with the bullet wound, but then he saw that the
woman looked nothing like Toby Ranger, even if the
female Fed had taken on a disguise. The woman
framed in the NVD's lens was short and very slim,
almost scrawny; she looked like a good gust of wind
would sweep her off the balcony. She had straight
dark hair that fell over her shoulders, and a bored expression on her face. She wore a blousy khaki shirt
and matching trousers.

The woman took a last drag from a cigarette and

flipped the butt over the balcony railing, leaning out to watch it wink down to the lawn below. Then she turned back to the sliding door.

Before she went through it, Bolan got a good look at the little automatic pistol in the belt holster at the small of her back. It was a partial confirmation, and for now it would have to do.

Still, he would have to go in soft, for a couple of reasons. First, he was not about to bust into the apartment with guns blazing on nothing but Corey James's information. Second, there was a possibility that Toby Ranger actually was inside, and Bolan would want to know her position before opening any fire. Third, this was civilian territory. If James's tip was good, Bolan could not risk the possibility of any innocent bystanders—and the apartment building was full of them—getting in the way of random lead.

Anticipating the situation, he had rigged soft. He wore an open-collar shirt under a stylishly cut sports jacket, and aviator-style glasses with slightly tinted lenses. The play might depend on a bit of role camouflage, the role of an American Intelligence agent gone bad.

Except that what was really going to go bad was some Italian terrorists' spring evening.

9

The inner door of the apartment building's entrance foyer was locked. On the wall to one side was a double-row of call buttons; the label on the one for apartment 4-D said "G. Feltrinelli."

Bolan pushed four of the other buttons at random. After a few seconds, a man's voice said something angry in Italian. Bolan tried the buttons again. This time the door buzzer sounded, and Bolan pushed through.

He took the elevator to the sixth floor and wedged a sand-filled ashtray in its door before taking the fire stairs back down two flights. The door to 4-D was at the end of the hall, offset maybe five feet from its neighbor opposite. That would provide slightly more privacy.

The bell was set into the middle of the door, and above it was the glass bead of a security peephole. Bolan pressed the bell, then put his thumb over the viewer.

He heard the noise of someone approaching the door, then silence. He pressed the bell again, heard it chime inside.

"Who is that?" It was the woman, speaking in elegant Italian.

Bolan rang the bell a third time.

Inside, a man's voice said something in Italian. The woman answered, and the man's voice rose in annoyance.

Bolan rang the bell once more, and this time the door opened a crack. It was held by a security chain.

The woman was shorter than Bolan had first thought, no more than five feet. She turned her dark face up to him, and scowled.

"I don't know you," she muttered.

"You know my boss."

"This boss, he has a name?"

"You know his name, too," he said in English.

The woman looked Bolan over, seemed uncertain. Behind her the man snapped out something. The woman tried to shut the door, but Bolan's foot was already wedged in it.

"What you want?" the woman said.

"Information."

"Go away."

Bolan laughed politely. "We can play this nice and quiet, like pros," he said pleasantly, "or we can wake up the neighbors. It's all the same to me. I don't have to live here."

The man said something else.

"Okay," the woman said quickly. Bolan moved his foot, and the door shut, then reopened a second later.

The apartment's furnishings were as impersonal as the building's design. There was a convertible sofa, all metal and vinyl, a couple of matching chairs, a few severe-looking coffee tables. On the other side of a counter top there was a pantry, and down a short hallway, off of which Bolan figured bedrooms opened, was the open door of a bathroom.

The guy was sitting in one of the chairs. He wore a sleeveless undershirt, and over it a shoulder holster containing a large pistol. On the table next to him was an ashtray full of butts and a water tumbler half-full of red wine. In front of him some old movie was showing on a black-and-white television, the sound barely audible.

"Who else is here?" If Bolan could keep the initiative, he might be able to make his play without guns coming into it. His jacket hid a silenced 9mm Beretta Brigadier in shoulder leather, but he hoped to keep it there. The weaponry that neither of these two were making much effort to conceal was a pretty clear signal as to who they were, but that did not give Bolan license to punish them for their crimes, real or imagined. He was here for information, not blood.

"Just us." The woman held up two fingers, unsure of her English.

The guy said something, and followed it with a healthy slug of the wine. His hand was unsteady.

"He wants to know who you are," the woman said.

"I work for Frank Edwards. That's all you have to know."

The woman translated. The guy frowned.

"Listen, there was a woman here yesterday, with Edwards. Taller than you, well built. Right?"

The woman nodded.

"Did she leave with him?"

The woman nodded again.

"Where did they go?"

The guy in the chair interrupted with a rapid burst of Italian. The woman started to answer, but he cut her off. Bolan tried to look uninterested. There was a magazine on one of the coffee tables, printed on cheap newsprint. It was in Italian, but on one side of the masthead was a hammer and sickle, and on the other a clenched fist raised in defiance. A photograph on the front page showed a fire-gutted automobile on a city street. Bolan leafed through it, feigning interest.

"He says you are not from Edwards," the woman said suddenly. She took a step back from Bolan. "He says if you are from Edwards, you not have to ask where he is."

"We had a meet set up," Bolan said patiently. "Who do you think gave me this address? I got held up, and now I have to know where he's moved on to."

The guy snapped out something, then drained the rest of the wine.

"He wants to know why you come the way you come, why you do not use the...what do you call it, the recognition code."

"Look." Bolan let anger color his voice. "I don't have time to play your little revolutionary games. I want to know where the hell Edwards is, and I want to know now."

The guy might not have understood, but he heard the tone. He slammed down his empty glass, hard enough to shatter it. Blood oozed from his palm, but he didn't seem to notice.

The guy was drunk, and that made him unpredictably dangerous. Bolan had to put him down, or the play would go right to hell. He took a step toward the guy.

The guy snarled something at Bolan, shifted his weight in the chair, and went for his gun.

Bolan threw the magazine in the guy's face.

The guy clawed at it, but by the time he'd gotten clear Bolan's own pistol was in his hand and leveled.

Bolan did not want to shoot—nor did he want to get shot. "Tell him to take it out with two fingers," Bolan said, not looking at the woman. "Tell him to drop it, and nobody gets hurt."

She never got it out.

The guy rolled out of the chair and came up on hands and knees, the pistol in his hand. He barked something, wine-red saliva spraying from his mouth, and drew a bead on Bolan.

The Beretta whispered, and a 9mm tumbler tore into the guy's right shoulder and tumbled him over on his side, the gun dropping from his nerveless fingers. He moaned once and lay still.

The woman's mouth formed a silent O, her eyes wild as a frightened doe's. Sure, she had just seen the difference between revolutionary theory and reality.

Reality was the red fluid leaking over the unconscious guy's dirty T-shirt.

The woman sunk into a chair, her eyes fixed on her partner's inert form. Bolan leaned over, grabbed her shoulders and shook her insistently. He could not afford to lose her now.

"Where did they go? Where did Edwards and the woman go?"

The girl stared at him through her wide eyes and shook her head.

"Do you know where they went?"

She nodded like a child.

"Tell me," Bolan said, his voice as even as he could make it.

"Yes." But she did not go on. Bolan shook her again, gently. "Water," the woman said. "Please."

He had just turned on the tap in the pantry when the gunshot exploded behind him.

Bolan twisted and the Beretta came back into his hand. The guy on the floor was sitting up, tracking his gun onto Bolan.

Bolan fired first, the Beretta sounding a soft murmur of death. A third eye appeared in the middle of the guy's forehead, and the guy lay down on his back again. A semiliquid mess of red and white and gray began to flow into the carpet beneath the back of his head.

The woman was slumped back in the chair. A dark stain was spreading on the khaki shirt between her small breasts. Her eyes were still open wide, as if imprinted in death with that final image of her own partner killing her to keep her from talking.

And in thirty seconds or less, that gunshot was going to bring a building full of people down on him. The numbers had just about run out.

Bolan used the ones left to check out the rest of the apartment—and came up empty.

From somewhere below on the fire stairs, Bolan heard excited voices and running footsteps. He went up instead. Between the fifth and sixth floors a man in a bathrobe grabbed his arm and said something in excited Italian. Bolan shook him off and continued on up.

The elevator was where he'd left it. The lobby was empty, although more agitated voices were audible from the open fire-stair door.

Across the Via del Gladiatori Bolan stopped and lit a cigarette. The first police car was just pulling up. The Italian cops had a pretty complete mug file of Red Brigades members. They would likely identify the two upstairs quickly, and after that the file would be closed. When someone did them the favor of killing off a couple of terrorists, the police were not about to waste a lot of time investigating.

The cigarette tasted stale, and Bolan ground it out. He had been close—damned close.

Now he was looking down a dead-end street that stopped in a brick wall.

10

Aaron Kurtzman punched a command into the computer terminal, and a line printer began chattering output at 80 characters per second. Kurtzman got up, absently brushing pipe ash from the front of his lab jacket, checked the first page, and smiled with satisfaction.

"It's all there," he said to the other two people in the Stony Man Farm War Room. "How Frederick Charon was going to juggle the inventory to replace the guidance-system prototype, how he was going to wash the money the Russians were supposed to pay him through Sir Philip Drummond, how he planned to peddle other items of interest." The Bear patted the terminal with his broad palm, as if it were a favorite pet. "Wonderful things, computers."

"What about the Frank Edwards angle, Aaron?" April Rose asked.

"Interesting—and more involved than we figured at first. It turns out that when Frank Edwards was a legitimate CIA operative, he had professional contact with both Sir Philip and his Russian control, a guy named Tartikov, who was nominally a protocol officer at the Russian Embassy in London. Nothing unusual about that, actually. Our agents and the

Soviets will collaborate once in a while, if it works to mutual advantage.''

Kurtzman fumbled his pipe out of his lab coat and began to stuff it with brown black tobacco. ''Anyway, as it happened, Edwards found out, purely by chance, that Sir Philip was a mole. Don't forget, Edwards was an extremely competent agent—and still is. Maybe Edwards was already thinking of selling out, but whatever, he kept the truth about Sir Philip under his hat. Then, when he went renegade, he used it to blackmail Sir Philip into siding with him.''

''How did he use Sir Philip?''

''Primarily as an intelligence source. Having a high-ranking official in the Ministry of Defence in your pocket could be pretty handy for a guy like Edwards.''

Kurtzman patted absently at his pockets for matches, until April tossed a folder across the table to him. ''Thanks. Okay, so Charon contacts the Russians. The Russians buy, and designate Sir Philip as the go-between. Then Sir Philip, recognizing a good deal when he sees one, tips off Edwards to Charon as a potential source of hi-tech gear—charging Edwards a hefty finder's fee, of course. Everyone is happy as larks.''

''Did Edwards buy from Charon?''

Kurtzman nodded at the printout. ''He put in one hell of an order—it's all right there, courtesy of the DonCo computer. Communications gear, sophisticated wiretaps and directional eavesdropping devices, computer hardware and software, weapons systems, cryptographics—you name it. All of it state-of-the-art, all of it top secret, all of it restricted to military and official agency usage.''

"But we were able to stop Charon before he shipped,'' April pointed out.

"Right,'' Kurtzman agreed. "But with the network Edwards has set up, he'll find someone to take Charon's place soon enough. The spokes are useful to us, but only as a way to find the hub. The way to kill this scheme once and for all is to stop Edwards.''

"And that's where Mack comes in,'' April said.

"And Toby.''

The third person in the War Room lowered himself into the chair next to April, rubbed at the bridge of his nose with two fingers. Though it was early evening, local time, none of them had gotten much sleep of late, and all were weary.

He had been born Giuseppe Androsepitone, but to an international audience he was known as Tommy Anders, The Ethnician. He was one of the most popular stand-up comedians in the U.S. and Europe, deriving his humor from good-natured ribbing of people's ethnic prejudices and preconceptions.

He was also an undercover federal agent.

That was why he had been brought to the War Room. Anders had been deceived, cruelly but necessarily.

For six months he had been made to believe that Toby Ranger, his partner all the way back to the days of Mack Bolan's War against the Mafia, had been cashiered for doubling.

"I'm not no ethnician,'' he said now—it was the signature line of his stand-up routine "—but I knew the kid wasn't any kind of turncoat. Say, what kind of ethnic is Ranger, anyway? The kid probably had it fixed, just like everyone else. Probably it used to be Rangeropoulos, Rangarelli, somethin' like that.'' It was a habit from childhood, one that had led to his cover profession; the wisecrack as a cover for nervousness and stress.

The only answer was from the line printer, spewing out the information that would damn Frederick Charon. After a while it stopped as well.

None of them spoke after that. There was nothing to talk about. There was nothing to do at all.

Except wait.

Kurtzman had gone to his billet for tobacco, and April Rose had managed to doze off in her chair, so it was Tommy Anders who spotted the red light flashing on the phone that sat alone on a table in the corner of the War Room. He leaped from his chair and reached it before it was able to flash twice more. Two tape recorders in the wall rack automatically started rolling, their "record" lights shining.

"Go," Anders said.

There was a pause, and then a woman's voice tinged with surprise said, "Tommy?"

"Hell God," Anders exploded. "Are you all right, Toby?"

"Yes. Listen." Composure, lost momentarily, returned. "I don't know how much time I've got."

Kurtzman came in, restuffing his pipe. When he saw Anders on that special phone, he froze, as if movement would break the precious connection.

April Rose had come awake and sat staring at Anders as well.

"Edwards and I are in Tripoli. Libya, not Lebanon." She rapped out an address. "It's coming down, the big push for his international 'black' intel net. The Valais meet was just the prelim. This one is the real thing."

"How are you fixed."

Electronic scrambler hash filled her pause. "I . . . I think I'm blown, Tommy. Edwards hasn't done anything yet, but I think he knows."

"Get out, Toby."

"Don't worry about me. There's still a few things to take care of."

"Mack. . . ."

"You tell Captain Hard to stay clear, Tommy. I'll take care of myself."

"Listen—"

"Can't. The numbers are up."

The line noise came up again, and then went dead.

Slow as a sleepwalker, Tommy Anders replaced the handset. He turned, looked blankly from April to Kurtzman. It was good to have Anders back in the War Room, by God, but there was nothing he could do now.

Kurtzman moved past him and began to rewind the tapes.

11

Mack Bolan did not know how many of the enemy had died at his hand. Though the men he had sent to their just reward probably numbered in the thousands, he was interested in results, not statistics. The Executioner did not "notch his gun."

He was not out to prove something, to reaffirm some fragile notion of manhood; nor were his campaigns half-cocked ego trips. The act of killing surely held no personal satisfaction for the man.

But yeah, make no mistake, men had died by his good right hand. He had faced the Armies of the Beast, the men who believed that if they could get in position to lord it over others they could assure their own well-being and prosperity.

Mack Bolan had shown them that all they assured were their own deaths.

There was blood on Bolan's hands, but his psyche was free of self-reproach. Whatever his guilty prey had suffered, they had inflicted ten times as greatly upon the innocent. These people against whom Bolan had pledged his life were nominally human beings, sure. But their morals and instincts were those of the savage. The dark warrior did not rue the fate of any man who had died at his hand. No ghosts came back to haunt his conscience.

And yet there had been casualties in the Bolan wars that the man grieved with all his being.

From the earliest days of the Mafia blitzes, there were men and women who recognized the value of the Executioner's radical methods. Some of these insisted on becoming active allies, on picking up the gun to stand on Mack Bolan's right hand.

Some of them had died.

There was the Death Squad, a ruthless unit comprised of nine of Bolan's old Vietnam comrades. Though disillusioned and demoralized by their countrymen's ambiguous rejection of them on their return, still they rallied around their one-time sergeant to once again put their lives on the line against that country's enemies. Seven of the nine in fact made that supreme sacrifice.

In New York, a lovely young woman named Evie Clifford gave shelter to a wounded Mack Bolan, and died a hideous tortured death at Mafia hands for her act of mercy. In New Jersey, a Vietnam vet named Bruno Tassily suffered the same horrific fate. Most recently, in Minneapolis, a lovely sensitive Mexican-American woman named Toni, sister to Bolan's Able Team comrade Rosario Blancanales, was savagely assaulted by a deranged rapist. But Toni, if badly scarred emotionally, at least remained among the living.

So Mack Bolan had come to accept that his simple presence could constitute the greatest danger to others. His war must be one of solitude, because for the man against whom a worldwide criminal organization was pitted, to make a friend was to create a potential victim.

It was any warrior's greatest vulnerability. To care for someone meant a chink in one's armor. The enemy could reach you through the one for whom you cared. Yet caring was something Bolan could not and would not give up, because caring, true caring on the personal level, was what distinguished the man from the vandals lined up against him. In the cosmic sense, the man had to care to fight.

And there were people who would fight along with him, whether he wished it or not.

People like Schwarz, Carl Lyons, Pol Blancanales—his Able Team, fellow fighters for the true freedoms. Like April Rose, who in a baptism in blood had come to his side. Like Leo Turrin, who had tiptoed closer to the edge of the abyss than any of them, operating undercover from the very belly of the Mafia monster. Like Phoenix Force, five men of action and success.

These were the good and the strong, and until they triumphed over the barbarians, Bolan would fight on. Each was a symbol, and a constant reminder of why his endless mile had to be walked. These people were with Mack Bolan always, the memories of those who had passed beyond, the spirit of those who lived to battle on.

Among them was one pure and large woman named Toby Ranger.

Fate had decreed that the path of Toby Ranger first intersect that of Mack Bolan during the early days of the Mafia wars. A need to replenish his campaign treasury had brought the man already referred to by the mob as "that bastard Bolan" to the desert mecca of Las Vegas, where he planned to liberate a quarter of a million dollars in cash illegally skimmed from the resort's gaming tables. What better way to finance the destruction of the criminal octopus than with the enemy's own dirty funds?

But as so often happened, the relatively simple mission quickly turned complex. The original strike, on a Mafia mountain hardsite above Lake Mead, turned up an unexpected dividend: the rescue of Carl Lyons, then an undercover cop on loan to the Justice Department. Lyons in turn led Bolan to Tommy Anders, not yet a federal agent, then playing his comedy act in a Vegas clubroom. Anders had refused to toe the mark for syndicate promoters and booking agents, and had paid for it with a beating and the promise of treatment far worse—until Mack Bolan took a hand.

Anders's back-up act was the Ranger Girls, a quartet of lovelies who took their name from their leader. The first time Bolan laid eyes on Toby Ranger he found it hard to pull them away. She was tall and blond and wide-eyed, and built like something out of a centerfold—the last part was apparent, since she wore peekaboo hotpants and a plunging see-through top that left little doubt about her vital statistics. With her three partners—Georgette Chebleu, Smiley Dublin, and Sally Palmer— Toby and the Ranger Girls sang, danced, snapped out one-liners, and played fifteen different instruments. Toby Ranger was the kind of dazzling combination of looks and talent that made any man, Mack Bolan included, sit up and take notice.

The Ranger Girls were good, damned good, and not only as show-biz performers. Only at the tag end of his Vegas vendetta, when Toby risked her cover and her life to help him out of what would have otherwise been an impossible situation, did Bolan get an inkling of the truth about the four women: they were soldiers of the same side as he. Under the show-girl cover, each was a federal agent. In fact, the gorgeous brunette French Canadian, Georgette, was fated to give up her life to her adopted country, reduced to something less than human through the insane torture of Fat Sal, the Mafia turkey doctor.

Toby Ranger remained a special memory to Mack Bolan. In those days the blitzer was doubly a wanted man, with a Mafia price on his head, and a federal warrant sworn against him. From this isolation, Toby became someone to whom he could turn, with whom he could even merge, however briefly. She was an agent of reaffirmation, that his fight and his survival *were* worthwhile. She enabled him to see beyond himself into that cosmic sprawl of uncommon magic.

When the theater of operations moved on to Detroit, Toby reentered the nightfighter's life. At first wary adversary, then reluctant ally, she became ardent, passionate lover. The life Bolan had created for himself, a life of war everlasting, contained little space for R & R. But he did relent to the extent of allowing the lady Fed to share his life for the few all-too-short days it took to travel to New Orleans, the next hellground. And for those days, Mack Bolan—

the complex man within the soldier—was entire and complete and, yeah, human once again.

They were not destined to come together again, not in that way. Yet Toby Ranger would always be a special leaf in Mack Bolan's epic book of life. He had known the woman in various roles, had appreciated and respected her in each. Perhaps he had even been a bit in love with her. But Bolan knew with perfect clarity that there was no room for love in the knife-edge world of a living dead man. To ignore that reality would be to deceive her—and himself as well.

They worked together again when the Executioner paid a visit to Hawaii, teaming with Lyons, Anders, and Smiley Dublin, all by that time SOGers, agents of the Sensitive Operations Group. When they were done, a proposed Mafia-Red Chinese link had died aborning. The five of them again combined talents in Nashville to bust up the music city drug operation of one Nick Copa. Finally, Toby's deep-cover penetration of Mafioso Tom Santelli's Maryland headquarters played a crucial role in Bolan's blitz on Baltimore, on the penultimate day of his one-week mop-up campaign that had ended the war on the mob.

But neither Bolan nor Toby had attempted to rekindle the physical closeness they had shared in Detroit. Yeah, they had been lovers, and always would be lovers, in the largest sense of the word. And maybe someday, in the best of all possible worlds toward which both of them had pledged their fight— in that world, maybe, they could be lovers in a personal sense as well.

But the future would see to itself. Mack Bolan was concerned only with the Now.

Now Toby Ranger was in the maw of the carnivore, and those rapacious jaws were about to clamp shut.

That she remained alive and entire was the merest hope. But it was hope he would not relinquish.

He would get to her in time. He would redeem the life now forfeit to terrorist whim.

And then he would unleash his own reign of terror, would leave the kingdom of the traitor Frank Edwards a scorched wasteland.

12

From what Mack Bolan could see, treason had been extremely profitable for Frank Edwards.

The luxurious villa was located west of downtown Tripoli, in the garden suburb of Giorgimpopoli. Though ninety-nine percent of the country of Libya was desert, Giorgimpopoli was temperate and Mediterranean. The curving street was lined with graceful date palms; a hedge of cool green foliage fronted the estate; beyond it, a wide expanse of irrigated lawn stretched to the house itself, a two-story European-style home that bespoke wealth and quiet elegance.

There was a little guardhouse near the break in the hedge that admitted the long arching driveway, but there was no gate. As near as Bolan could tell, the middle-aged uniformed man who occupied it was unarmed. He was there for courtesy, not security; it was likely he did not even know what his boss did to support this expensive life-style.

Framed in the lens of the Litton Night Scope, the guard yawned. Likely he was nearing the tail end of his graveyard shift. Dawn was maybe an hour away.

Bolan slumped lower in the seat of the Jaguar sedan, parked across from the villa. He had been there for perhaps twenty minutes; in that time the guard's yawn was the most activity he'd seen.

This was no hardsite, that was certain. It was what it appeared to be, the expansive home of a wealthy man, secure in his station in life and his personal safety from unwanted intruders. Inside, Frank Edwards would have bodyguards, would have a garage full of cars; those were elementary precautions for a man in his dirty business. But in Libya, there was hardly any need for Edwards to surround himself with a private army.

No other country in the world had so closely identified itself with the terrorist cause. No other country had thrown open its arms as widely to embrace the violent hordes.

In 1969, Colonel Muammar al-Khaddafi had led a military coup. He remained to this day head of the Revolutionary Command Council, prime minister, minister of defense, and commander in chief. His support of terrorism was documented fact. Khaddafi had provided money, training, and arms to virtually every terrorist group in the world, including Nicaragua's Sandinistas, the IRA Provisional Army, armed revolutionary groups in Egypt and the Sudan, and Muslim rebels in the Philippines. With proven oil reserves of 28 *billion* barrels, and complete control over how to spend the profits from this vast ocean of petroleum, Khaddafi was in a unique position.

He had been using that position from the past ten years—to subsidize death.

The late Egyptian President Anwar Sadat, himself the victim of fanatics' guns, once called Khaddafi "a vicious criminal, 100 percent sick and possessed of a demon." The president of Sudan, Gaafer Mohammed Numeiry, noted that Khaddafi had "a split personality—both evil." Other observers felt the two African leaders' descriptions were admirably restrained.

So it was little wonder that Frank Edwards felt secure under Khaddafi's wing. Libya, Bolan knew full well, would be the perfect place for Edwards to base his "black" CIA. His experience, contacts, and expertise, combined with Khaddafi's sponsorship, would give the network almost quasi-governmental status.

If Edwards succeeded, the result would be awesome, almost unbelievable—but inescapable fact: the terrorist network would have an intelligence capacity nearly equal to that of the great free nations.

Already the wheels were in motion. The only way left to destroy the corpus of the scheme was to cut out its heart.

Frank Edwards had to be neutralized, and the Executioner was itching to apply his own unique method of neutralization.

The world was a precariously balanced entity, Bolan knew. Yet in some way, there was a force—call it destiny, cosmic influence, the hand of a greater consciousness—a force that worked to preserve that balance.

In a sterile apartment in Rome, a young woman needlessly dies, the last link to another young woman's postexistence. But then the other woman's voice is heard, the link reappears, and the world is in balance again.

When Bolan had finally contacted Aaron Kurtzman at the Stony Man Farm base, less than six hours before, Toby's call had already set wheels a-turning. U.S. military aircraft did not enter Libyan airspace, by mutual agreement; in fact, it had not been so long before that under orders from Khaddafi, Libyan fighters had fired on American jets flying in *international* airspace over the nearby Gulf of Sidra. Two planes had gone down—but they sure as hell had not belonged to the U.S.

However, several American oil companies maintained exploitation and development contracts with Khaddafi. It would come as no surprise to anyone to learn that certain people associated with one or more of these companies and stationed in Libya had certain quasi-official connections with American Intelligence. It was that channel that Kurtzman pursued.

The pilot of the unmarked twin-engine passenger jet had been young, professional, an excellent aviator, and admirably taciturn. He had spoken exactly three sentences to Bolan: "Good evening, sir," "Fifteen minutes to landing, sir," and "Good luck, sir." Between the first and the second, Bolan caught a couple of hours of combat sleep. When he awoke the pain in his shoulder was down to a dull throb that was merely bothersome.

The vague silhouette of a pipe-head pumping station was visible near the private desert airstrip where they'd landed. The man in the Nebraska Cornhuskers sweatshirt standing beside the open trunk of the Jaguar had less to say than the pilot. He shone a flashlight over the trunk's contents. Bolan looked them over and nodded. It would do.

It would have to.

The man in the sweatshirt slammed the trunk, handed Bolan the keys, and slipped into darkness. Seconds later the Jaguar's headlights were slashing across the sandy wasteland, pointed north.

Now, seated in the luxury vehicle across from the House that Betrayal Built, Bolan felt refreshed and ready. At that hour just before dawn, most men's biological clocks tick their slowest, and for that reason it would have been a good time for a strike. But everything else dictated against it.

Frank Edwards was no superstitious Mafia *capo*, nor a fanatic but ill-trained terrorist gunman. He had survived years of espionage work, followed by a meteorological climb on the edge of the shadow world of international violence, because he was smart enough to know he was always living on the heartbeat. The safety of this Tripoli retreat was relative, and Frank Edwards would know that.

The guy was playing on his home court, and if Bolan tried some crazy-haired one-man cavalry charge into the midst of it, he'd never get near the renegade agent.

There was another, although secondary, consideration: the safety of one Toby Ranger.

Bolan's primary mission was to stop Edwards, and if he succeeded there would be one less threat to the gentle people everywhere.

And if he succeeded in saving Toby's lovely butt at the same time, so much the better.

Until it was proven absolutely impossible, Bolan would aspire to achieve both goals.

So now it was time for planning, surveillance,

logistics. That house across the street—any house—was like a living organism, and in time would reveal its secrets. That was all the edge Bolan could hope for.

As it turned out, he got a good deal more.

13

The three men moved like a drill team that had re-hearsed this routine so many times it was second nature. Two of them came around the Mercedes diesel sedan, sliding into front and back seat with movement so identical they could have been wired in tandem. As the first guy fired up the ignition, the one standing shoulder-to-shoulder with the woman pushed her into the back of the sedan from the house side, slid in beside her to sandwich her against his partner.

By the time they had started down the villa's curving driveway, Bolan had the Jag started. The Night Vision Goggles were on the dashboard, and pulling the head strap on and comfortably positioning the leather-covered foam face cushion took only a second or two. He had preadjusted the eyepiece focus, eye separation, tilt and eye relief, and range focus, and needed only to flick on the power switch under the left tube.

The Litton M-802 goggles were the stablemate of the Pocket Scope, essentially two second-generation passive image intensifiers set in tandem as a self-contained binocular. The disadvantage of the Pocket Scope was the variable magnification of its zoom lens; the goggles were fixed at 1X, or unity. But the goggles allowed hands-free operation ideally suited for, among other things, driving.

And it looked like Bolan had some driving to do.

The Mercedes came out of the drive with lights doused and turned north, the direction Bolan was facing. The NVD made the interior as visible to Bolan as if the dome light had been lit.

Her blond hair was disheveled, and what Bolan could see of her face was set in a hard mask that could have been frustration, anger—or pain. But Bolan would have made her out if she were laughing and bald.

It was Toby Ranger, for sure.

Someone was sending her for a ride. Bolan meant to make certain it was not her last one.

Ahead of him the Mercedes's taillights came on and began immediately to recede.

Bolan let the Jag gently idle.

Five beats later, a second vehicle came out of the villa's driveway, a sleek-lined Saab Turbo carrying two men. It turned after the Mercedes.

Sure, a tag car was elementary tradecraft. Especially when the lead vehicle was carrying precious cargo.

Bolan eased the Jag into the parade, keeping the headlights off. With the Litton goggles, the brightness control automatically adjusting to streetlights, oncoming vehicles, and other changes in itensity, his night vision without lights was better than the other drivers' with.

Bolan had recognized one of them, one of the

sandwich men in the back of the Mercedes. His name was T.W. Hansen, and he was one of the five suspect-terminations on the list that had also included Corey James, the Valais chalet houseman. Until just three weeks before, Hansen had been a Master Sergeant in the Special Forces, with fourteen years of service and a record of several successfully completed and sensitive intelligence-related "hard" missions. Then he had suddenly turned up AWOL.

It looked like his status would have to be upgraded to "Deserted."

Bolan's task was simple, and yet breathtakingly complex. All he had to do was stop two powerful vehicles, overcome the objections of five experienced and no doubt armed fighting men, and liberate one highly compromised undercover agent without catching her in the cross fire. And accomplish it all on terrain with which he was only vaguely familiar.

He could not allow the two cars to reach their destination; the play had to be on neutral territory. But as long as they kept moving, Bolan could be reasonably sure that Toby would remain in one piece. His hunch was that Toby's cover had been blown too recently for them to have milked her of all the valuable information she could reveal. If that were the case—and Bolan had to believe it was—they were headed for a facility more isolated than the Giorgimpopoli villa.

Somewhere where her screams of anguish would go unheard.

They entered the more congested part of Tripoli; even at this early hour traffic had picked up. Bolan risked the headlights and blended into the flow, two cars behind the Saab tail car. At the coast highway, the Saab turned right, to the east. On the left Bolan passed the drying flats of a marine salt distillery. A little farther on was the harbor, and opposite it the mosques of Gurgi and Karamanli, the marble triumphal arch of Marcus Aurelius.

The city behind them, they passed through a shanty town, vague figures already stirring in the predawn darkness. Beyond it the Saab turned back south. Bolan doused the lights again and followed.

He was pretty sure now where the two-car caravan was heading.

Back in the early days of his military service, then-Sergeant Mack Bolan had been aboard a troop transport plane that had landed at Wheelus Air Base for service and refueling. With an hour or so to kill, a couple of Sergeant Bolan's squad had anted up a couple of cartons of American smokes and talked him into trading them for the use of a Jeep for a little sightseeing. They had not had time to go far, but Bolan had a fair recall of the area around the USAF base which they had managed to take in.

Wheelus had been closed since 1970; Khaddafi had kicked out the American "imperialist warmongers" soon after he forcibly grabbed the reins of power. But the physical plant was still mostly intact: runways, hangars, maintenance shops, billets, offices.

It could provide a turnkey base for Frank Edwards's "black" CIA.

The gate of Wheelus could be no more than a couple of miles farther on. Here the two-lane road ran straight as an arrow through scrub-grass plain, climbing a slight rise that might provide the last cover for Bolan's play. The two cars ahead of him had tightened to within six lengths of each other, running about fifty miles per hour through the black-gray of predawn.

Numbers moved backward in Bolan's head, and ran out.

Bolan tromped down on the gas of his darkened vehicle, and the Jaguar leaped at the rear of the car ahead. The wheelman of the tag car was good at his work, and the Saab was fully the Jag's equal in acceleration and speed. But the guy found himself sandwiched, with nowhere to go.

His partner twisted in the passenger seat, and automatic weapons fire splattered through the louvered rear window of the Saab. One end of the spoiler wing tore loose and banged across body metal in a shower of sparks. But by then Bolan had already pulled up on the driver's side.

His image eerily enhanced by the Night Vision Goggles, the wheelman was momentarily profiled through the Jag's passenger window. Bolan saw the guy start to wrench the wheel over hard, setting to broadside the Jag.

He never finished the motion.

The Beretta 93R machine pistol in Bolan's right hand chattered out a three-round burst of 9mm tumblers; though both cars were careening down the road, the range from the pistol's muzzle to the wheelman's head was no more than ten feet.

At the same moment Bolan floored the Jag. The

British sedan leapt forward like it had been goosed.

The Saab caught the Jag's left rear quarter-panel, and Bolan steered one-handed against the fishtail skid. A spasm of protesting pain shot through his left shoulder, but then the Beretta was in his lap and he was able to get both hands on the wheel again.

The two guys in the Saab weren't so lucky.

In the rearview mirror, Bolan saw the tag car tear diagonally across the road, momentarily going airborne as it cleared the shoulder. When it hit, the right front corner seemed to catch, and the car did a one-and-a-half flip through midair before landing on its roof.

Scant seconds had passed since Bolan had made his move.

The driver of the big Mercedes was milking it for all the speed it had, but the boxy diesel machine was designed for reliability, not racing. Bolan's headlights were on now, high beams cutting a trail to the lead vehicle. It took the Jag only a heartbeat to close the thirty yards to it.

One of the baby-sitters in the back seat twisted out the window, an M-16 cradled in his arms. Angry 5.56mm whizzers hemstitched starbursts across the Jag's windshield.

Bolan slumped in the contoured seat and eased more speed out of the rig. A moment later he felt the substantial thump of his front end tagging the Mercedes, heard the distinctive whine of tearing body metal.

The weapon's chatter stopped.

Bolan rose, dropped back ten feet to get the angle,

and put three-round bursts into each of the Mercedes's rear tires. The vehicle settled down on its haunches, one tire throwing a ragged strip of rubber off into the night.

Bolan cranked the wheel hard, snaked the Jag around the crippled Mercedes, then tapped the brake and pulled the wheel all the way around with his good right arm. The car eeled around in a perfect one-eighty. Leaving the high-beam headlights on, Bolan was EVA almost before the skid was over.

The Uzi hung from a lanyard around Bolan's neck. He sprayed a line of 9mm slugs across the front of the Mercedes, the big sedan still lumping toward him. Headlights blinked out in a shower of glass shards, and superheated steam wheezed from the punctured radiator.

Answering fire raked the Jag. But by then Bolan was already circling for the Mercedes. In the black-suit he was nearly one with the encompassing night, but the NVD goggles revealed the other four players in this game of death as clear as daylight.

Three of the sedan's four doors were open wide. From the far side of the back seat, Toby Ranger and the Green Beret deserter T.W. Hansen had pulled out. Hansen was dragging her roughly by one arm into the scrub grass. Despite the unexpected ambush, the guy had stuck with his primary assignment.

The driver and his partner were crouched behind the cover of the other doors, frantically searching the dark for a target.

They were looking in the wrong direction.

From off to the side, the Uzi spoke again, the hider

concealing any revealing muzzle flash. The upper half of the driver's body punched back inside, sprawling him across the front seat. His partner reacted automatically and sensibly, diving across the deck for the cover of the other side.

A precise line of 9mm hollow-points helped him on his way.

A harsh voice broke the momentary silence. "Hold it! You move and the woman dies!"

T.W. Hansen was maybe fifty feet into the scrub grass. He held Toby Ranger's arm in the vise grip of his left hand, and an Ingram M-10 machine pistol in his right.

Bolan let the Uzi hang free from its lanyard, unsheathed the big Beretta, setting the selector on single-shot.

The NVD goggles revealed a pulpy bruise on one side of Toby Ranger's forehead. Her eyes seemed half-closed.

"Show yourself, hands empty," Hansen called. "You do it, right now."

It was the odds-on gamble for the tall professional soldier, but Lady Luck was riding with the Executioner.

Lady Luck, and the lady named Ranger.

Toby moved suddenly, wrenching hard enough to force Hansen to take a step to keep his balance, yet not hard enough to break his grip. In reaction Hansen jerked her back toward him, and Toby stumbled to one knee.

The target was already framed over the Beretta's sight.

Bolan squeezed off the single round, and the heavy 9mm bonecrusher flashed through the night, seeking impediment, and found it in the middle of Hansen's forehead, punching him away and onto his back.

When Bolan reached him his eyes were open, and he was still holding Toby in lifeless fingers.

Toby pulled free. She looked up at Bolan, gasped, and got her hands around the fallen Ingram.

She leveled the weapon on Bolan's midsection. "One more step, Mister Whoever-You-Are," she said. She was obviously hurting, and this was costing her more pain. "One more step, and you are stew-meat."

Only then did Bolan realize that in the Night Vision Goggles, with their twin extruded vision tubes, he must have looked like some kind of bug-eyed apparition from someplace highly unpleasant.

He pulled the goggles off, keeping both hands visible.

The Ingram in Toby's hand lowered, forgotten.

"Captain Cavalry," she breathed. "In the flesh." She managed to stand. "If you aren't a sight for sore eyes."

Toby tried to take a step toward him and pitched forward instead. Bolan caught her soft bulk against his chest and lowered her gently back to the grass.

14

It was a reunion, for sure. But the popping of champagne corks and the rehashing of old times would have to wait.

Toby was out, but she didn't seem to be badly hurt. The laceration on her forehead was the only visible sign of abuse. Bolan's hard fingers, moments before gripped around gunmetal, took her wrist with infinite gentleness. The pulse was regular and strong, and her breathing, though a little ragged, was steady.

Bolan stripped off Hansen's jacket and covered Toby with it, then replaced the Night Vision Goggles in position and moved out along his backtrack.

The Saab Turbo was a ruggedly constructed machine, built to take even the kind of roll this car had endured without major structural damage. The same was not true of the human body. The shotgun rider was slumped out of his seat belt into what had been the roof, his head bent over at nearly a ninety-degree angle to his torso, his neck snapped like a wishbone. The top of the driver's head was not even there, except as a gory smear on the upholstery; Bolan's three-round burst had obviously found a tight grouping in its target.

When he got back, Toby was sitting up.

"What's broken?" Bolan's tone was gruff. There were too many other things he really wanted to say and ask, but right now there was only time for business.

Sooner or later—the later the better—Frank Edwards was going to miss his five hardboys.

"Nothing." She took the hand he offered, let him pull her to her feet. "I'm okay, Captain Quick, honest Injun."

In the Jaguar he dug a first-aid kit from a pack. He swabbed the forehead wound with an antiseptic towelette; once the dried blood was gone it didn't look too bad, as if someone had hit her a glancing blow with a gun barrel or a hand on which a ring was worn. Bolan squeezed antibiotic ointment from a tube, smeared it over the cut, covered it with a small adhesive compress.

When he was finished, Toby twisted the rearview mirror to where she could get a look at herself. She made a half-hearted attempt to push tangled blond hair into some kind of order, then gave it up and slumped back into the seat.

"I'm beat, Captain Hard," she said, her usual sardonic tone thin and forced now. "The last thirty-six hours have been something of a drain—to say the least."

"Toby," Bolan said, gently but firmly. "I need to have everything you can give me, and I need it now."

Immediately she sat up straighter. "I'm down, but I didn't say I was out. From here on it's a two-pronged blitz, Captain Courageous."

Bolan let that pass. Sure, Toby had proven herself

on the field of battle more than once, and he had no
theoretical objection to her fighting at his side. He
had put the days of purely solo warfare behind him
for good when he had accepted the support and sanction of the man in the Oval Office. Still, though he
could push it to the back of his mind, what he'd once
had with Toby would always be there, and a part of
his concentration, no matter how minor, would be
concerned with her safety.

A situational decision could be made when they
reached the situation.

"Are you blown, Toby?" Bolan asked.

"I think so. With Edwards it's not always easy to
tell where you're at. He's sharp, Mack," she said
seriously. "My cover was bound to unravel sooner or
later. First of all, I know he checked my record out
all the way back to Adam. Believe it or not, the guy
still has an ear to the CIA ground. Sure, he didn't
learn anything that proved I hadn't gone renegade
like him, but up until then I was too damn clean. For
a guy with his sensitive nose, it would have smelled
fishy."

Toby brushed absently at a grass stain. She was
wearing a jump suit of white parachute cloth, cut to
accentuate the swelling curve of her hips, the front
zipper pulled low enough to expose the valley of her
full breasts. "Second, he caught me yesterday—God,
it seems like a week ago—in Valais, making contact
with Stony Man base. Making the call was a risk, but
I thought it likely I was already blown, and what Edwards had planned needed to be stopped pronto. He
didn't really hear anything—but it was sort of suspi-

cious, from his point of view. For sure he thought I was calling the States.''

"Do all of his people know you're on the outs?"

"Probably not. It was—" she glanced at her watch "—only about an hour ago. Hansen and his boys busted into my room, told me to dress, and hustled me out. They claimed the boss wanted me on ice for a while, but I was afraid Edwards had given them orders to interrogate as well.''

Suddenly she shuddered involuntarily. "Edwards told me a story once, soon after I hooked up with him—I don't know if he was trying to impress me or intimidate me. He said that one of the African tinhorn dictators had a special way of questioning prisoners to get them to give him the names of opposition sympathizers. The prisoner was strapped down on his back so he could only lift his head, and a rat was placed on his stomach, and over the rat a glass bowl. Then the bowl was heated. The rat only had one way out. Edwards said if the prisoner didn't pass out, he could watch the rat eat its way through his guts.''

"Easy," Bolan said gently. "That's enough.''

Toby squared her shoulders, as if shaking off the image. "Anyway, thinking about that, being awakened in the dark and so on, I didn't go quietly at first." She touched at the dressing on her forehead. "That's how I got the souvenir.''

"So as far as most of Edwards's cadre know, you're still one of the gang?"

"Possibly. Even probably. Today is another big day for Edwards. I don't think he'd want the word to get out about any kind of trouble.''

"What's going down, Toby?"

"Exactly what I thought when I made contact yesterday. Edwards is organizing an international intelligence agency with loyalties only to the highest bidders. It's incredible, but I'm afraid the guy can make it work—and on a far greater scale than we ever suspected. For example, even though the word has gone out to every friendly intelligence agency in the world that Edwards is believed guilty of treasonous activities and no longer has any official CIA status, the guy can still tap into nearly all of his old sources."

"Through other traitors still in place?"

"No, Mack. That's the hell of it. Through loyal, committed operatives. You see, that whole shadowland they call espionage is built on a foundation of suspicion and intrigue. Edwards has let it be leaked to a select few on the inside that he was never fired from the agency at all; it was all a scam to get an operative into Libya and buddy-buddy with Khaddafi. And in a crazy kind of way it could make sense."

Sure, Bolan thought, in a topsy-turvy world where a government agent could become a turncoat representing himself as an agent, anything made sense, if you spent enough time trying to figure it out, trying to pigeonhole it into one of the cubicles of rational experience. But there was nothing rational about international terrorism, and those like Edwards who shored it up. Edwards was a traitor, and by proxy a mass murderer. And all the rationalization in the world was not going to neutralize him.

Direct action was the only response to the Frank Edwardses of the world, the kind of direct action that the Executioner held a patent on.

"Edwards has a broad base of direct support as well," Toby went on. "He already has commitments with agents from around the world. Men like himself, willing to give up any idea of allegiance, except to profit. He's been in contact with people in the British MI5, the French SDECE, the Israeli Shin Bet, the German BND. And he's not limiting himself to the Western allies, either. He's also hooked up with agents of the KGB, the Social Affairs Department of Red China, and Castro's DGI."

Incredible, for sure. Once his network was set up, he would be in a position to subvert the intelligence activities of every major power in the world. The precarious balance of the rock of world peace would go straight to hell, and when it toppled it would start an avalanche that could only end in total destruction.

"Mack!" The alarm in her tone cut into his reflections. Instinctively his fist tightened on the Beretta.

But Toby was looking at the chest of the nightsuit. The black material was stained with something darker.

"You're hit," Toby said.

Bolan unzipped the front flap. "Just grazed. It happened yesterday." But the compress over the exit wound was soaked with fresh blood.

"Grazed?" Toby echoed skeptically.

Bolan got out a fresh field bandage and slapped it over the old one. But again the pain in the torn muscle had become sharper; no doubt the firefight just past had not done it any good.

"I'm all right," Bolan said. He rezipped the outfit, but Toby was still staring at the bloodspot. "How is Edwards financing this scheme?"

Toby turned her frown on Bolan again. "Several sources. His first scheme, after he split with the CIA, involved brokering illegally exported arms, mostly American-made, to terrorists and various other sorts of criminals. The weapons—everything from automatic pistols to heat-seeking missiles—were smuggled to London. That was where Sir Philip Drummond came in. He made sure that there was either storage in the International Zone at Heathrow Airport, which meant no customs inspection, or that if there did have to be an inspection, the customs agents were bought off or fixed in some other way. Meanwhile, Edwards would use his connections to doctor up an end-users' certificate, which is a document by one government friendly to the U.S. that states that armament stored in another country had been duly and legally purchased. Of course, the real destination was never the one that was registered, but one of Edwards's warehouses instead. The weapons business is highly profitable. Edwards marks up the goods three or four hundred percent, depending on the buyer and the merchandise."

Toby shook her head, almost sadly. "I got to know the guy a little, Mack. He is one of the most frightening men I've ever met, because to him it's as if it's just an exercise in deception and wheeling-dealing, a game at which he has grown expert. He knows intellectually that people are dying because of it, but emotionally he is completely aloof.''

It was the ultimate ego trip, sure. The notion that the world is composed of You and Everyone Else, because no one can touch you in deceit and manipulation. Except Edwards was wrong: he would be touched all right, and touched hard.

"I think Edwards has also received seed money from some of the wealthier terrorist groups. We know that before he began to set up his spy net, eyewitnesses placed him at the scene of several high-level meetings among Arab radical factions. At least a dozen European assassinations have been pinned on them in the past two years, and one or two of the earlier ones may have been Edwards's personal work. Now some of those groups are anteing up seed money.''

"So it all ties in.''

"Even more than we thought,'' Toby added. "It turns out that Edwards even has quasi-official status. Nominally, the reason he is in Tripoli is to train a class of Libyan intellectuals in espionage technique, and to design and start up an intelligence agency for Khaddafi. Of course, Khaddafi knows this is a cover for Edwards's own ambitions, but he doesn't particularly care. He'll be one of Edwards's best customers, and he'll even get a discount.''

Bolan pressed in the Jag's dashboard lighter and fished out a cigarette. "I figured he's using Wheelus as a base.''

"That's right,'' Toby confirmed. "His primary communication and computer data-bank facility is there, and his own planes fly out of the old base. He's also got his largest illegal-weapons warehouse there too, in an old quartermaster corps facility—and right now it's filled with inventory.''

"Can you sketch me a layout of the base, Toby?"

"You bet, Captain Grim."

She found paper and pen in the sedan's glove box and began to rough out a schematic as Bolan asked, "How long before Edwards misses Hansen?"

"I'm not sure. Hansen wouldn't necessarily check in just to tell Edwards we had reached Wheelus, not unless something was wrong. But there's a good chance that the next one of Edwards's group to pass this way is going to recognize those two wrecked cars, investigate, and blow the whistle. It's still pretty early; with luck we might have a couple of hours."

"That could be all we need."

Toby looked across the seat at him and frowned, like she already knew the answer to the question she was about to ask. "Now wait a minute, Captain Incredible. Are you thinking of taking him on by yourself?"

"Toby, Frank Edwards can't be touched through official channels. Technically, he hasn't been charged with any crime by American authorities, because to do so would open some top-secret cans of worms. Technically, he's outside the reach and authority of our law, anyway. Technically, no American agent or law officer has any official status in Libya."

"Yeah," Toby Ranger said sarcastically, "and

technically, the Mafia never existed. If you go strictly by the book, that is.''

''Which is why—''

''Which is why,'' Toby interrupted, ''we're going by the book *you* wrote. It's just like the bad old days, isn't it, Captain Tough? Hit 'n' git, the hellfire storm, all of it. Call it 'Blitzing the Baddies, by Captain Death.' ''

Mack Bolan did not smile. ''I'll need intel, Toby. With cars and bodies littering that field, we could go on the heartbeat any second.''

''Mack, with that arm. . .the chances. . . .'' She bit at her lip. You did not start thinking chances at a time like this.

''The layout at the villa,'' Bolan pressed. ''Number and positioning of security layout, anything else you can give me.''

Toby sighed. ''You got it, Captain Stubborn.'' But then her wry smile turned into a pained drawn expression, as if all the tension of the past six months of living undercover, acting a role for the Oscar Award that was life or death, had finally become frighteningly real to her.

''Mack,'' she said, in a voice gone suddenly little-girl. She leaned across, and he let her come into his arms. There was nothing sexual about it; it was the need of two people to feel for a few moments a human touch, in the midst of the all-too-inhuman world in which they found themselves so often. He felt the warm wetness of her tears soaking through the elastic material of the blacksuit.

''It's okay,'' he told her in an incredibly soft voice.

"Damn it," Toby sobbed, and Bolan knew she was referring to nothing and everything. "Just damn it."

Too quickly the moment was over. So few, those moments, so far between—and so essential.

As essential as the need to stop Frank Edwards.

Toby was sitting across the seat again, her eyes red but dry. "I'm ready," she said, calmly, levelly.

East across the flat grassy plain, dirty gray fingers of dawn licked away the night sky. Another day, and another long yard in the Executioner's endless Third Mile of War.

But Bolan nodded. He was ready as well.

15

Mack Bolan lay without breathing on the floor in front of the Jag's rear seat, his still form hidden beneath a rough wool blanket. The car cruised to a stop, and Bolan heard the sound of boot heels on pavement as the gateman came over.

Bolan tensed, holding the charged Uzi in ready position. If Toby's cover had been blown completely off and the guard blew the whistle on her now, the scene was going to go rapidly hard.

"Accident?" The gateman's voice came from the rig's passenger side. Its tone was casual.

"Somewhere along the line," Toby replied just as lightly. "It was like that when I left Frank's place."

"A Jag, huh," he heard the gateman say rhetorically. "I haven't seen this one around before."

Either the guy was looking for conversation to break up the monotony of duty—or he was stalling for time.

"I guess Frank just picked it up. Probably at a discount because of the dent, if I know Frank."

The gateman laughed. "Frank knows the value of a buck, that's for sure."

"Just like the rest of us, huh?"

"Right you are, Toby. Listen, what's up?"

In the background, Bolan could hear the Doppler effect of an approaching plane.

"That goddamned tag car was on its way to pick up some guy named Sid Bryant. That's probably his flight coming in now," she whispered to Bolan.

"Who is he?"

"Used to be FBI, but he's been freelancing around Europe and the Middle East for the past couple of years. Frank's never met him, I guess, but he'd got the credentials and recommendations."

"Coming in for the big meet?"

"No, that's just coincidence. He'll be there, I guess, but mainly Frank is just checking him out."

Toby shifted the sedan into gear. "Take it easy, Toby," the gateman called as she moved on into the one-time USAF base turned terrorist nerve center.

Bolan let out breath and loosened his death grip on the Uzi.

He had changed out of the midnight suit and into light cotton twill slacks, a khaki safari shirt, and dark glasses. In the front right-hand pocket of the slacks was stowed a C.O.P. (Compact Off-Duty Police), Inc. SS-1 four-barrel hideaway pistol, in .357 Magnum.

The Jaguar rolled to a smooth stop. From the sound of the engines as they were killed, the plane was close by. The Jag's door opened, slammed again.

"How they hanging, Toby?" a man's voice asked.

"Keep your mind on flying, Jerry." Toby's tone was just as bantering. "Are you Bryant?" she asked after a pause.

A different man answered, "That's right."

"Your chariot awaits, chum."

Both front doors opened, and the Jag's suspension shifted under the weight of Toby and Bryant. The car started up again, swung around in a U-turn. It slowed long enough for Bolan to hear the gateman's, "Later, Toby," then sped up again.

"Welcome to Tripoli, Bryant," Toby said casually.

Bolan slipped out from under the blanket and rose silently to his knees, bringing up the Uzi.

Bryant had started to murmur a response to Toby's apparent pleasantry when the barrel of the Uzi drilled into the base of his skull.

"You've got two choices, Bryant," Bolan said into the guy's ear, his voice sharp and cold as an icicle. "If you keep your eyes straight ahead and your hands in sight, you get a long walk back from the desert. If you even twitch, you get your brains all over the dashboard."

"I guess I've got a long walk coming up," Bryant said expressionlessly.

Understanding the enemy, in everything from moti-
vation to method, was an invaluable aid, Bolan had
learned—it was the edge that kept a man living. So
from the moment he had received in London from
Aaron Kurtzman at Stony Man Farm the telexed
précis of Frank Edwards's dossier, he had budgeted a
significant portion of his available waking time while
in transit to studying, analyzing, and extrapolating
strengths, weaknesses, causality, technique. By
applying his vast storehouse of experiential knowledge of the human animal, Bolan was able to virtually open the lid of the man and examine the works
inside.

Frank Edwards, age 38. Born Manchester, New
Hampshire, to Earl Edwards, grocery wholesaler,
and Bernice Edwards, high-school teacher. Educated
in public grammar and high schools; two-year letter-
man in football and track, vice-president of the student council, honor roll academically. B.A. degree
from Yale University; dual major in history and
political science, upper-level courses in psychology,
sociology, Spanish, German. Four years army
ROTC. Grade level of 73rd percentile, i.e. academically above average but not extraordinary.

The bare-bones outline of Edwards's post-graduate career went like this: Commissioned a 2nd Lieutenant, U.S. Army, assigned to military intelligence. Stationed in Saigon for twenty months during the height of the Vietnam War. Usual citations, honorable discharge six months before scheduled expiration of enlistment at administrative request, discharge rank of captain.

Joined the Central Intelligence Agency on discharge, posted to Langley for training. Subsequent postings to Caracas, Malaysia, Belgrade, Bonn, Paris. Chief of Middle East Section, HQ in Beirut, when his service was terminated. Total agency service: fourteen years, four months.

The anecdotal material that the Bear had appended to the dossier fleshed out the skeletal, and fairly typical, description of one agent's career—and revealed that Edwards was hardly typical at all.

The CIA, Bolan knew, was not some sort of arcane secret society, approaching potential agents in the dead of night, swearing them to secrecy and offering them a James Bondian life of excitement and high adventure. Sure, of necessity there was a certain covertness to the agency's activities, and the mental and physical prerequisites for agents were extremely rigorous, designed to screen out all but the very best. But the CIA hired much like any other corporation, interviewing applicants on college campuses for example, as openly as General Motors.

Occasionally, if in the course of his work a field agent encounters a particularly promising candidate, he might recommend he apply. This was the case with

Frank Edwards, who during his military stretch came in normal contact with the head of the CIA's Saigon station. It was Edwards's successful application that led to his early discharge from regular military service.

A senior CIA field agent is given a great deal of autonomy; that was the reason for the meticulous screening procedure through which Edwards passed with flying colors. Although an agent enjoys the resources of the world's finest intelligence agency, he is also expected to develop and exploit his own sources. His primary mandate is explicit, and he is often given specific assignments, but he may also act on his own initiative if the contingencies of the moment demand it. In the words of William Colby, one of the CIA directors under whom Edwards worked: "It is the function of an agent, in the proper use of the situation, to maneuver himself into a situation by his own wits."

Quite simply, Frank Edwards made an excellent spy. He was intelligent, cool-headed, resourceful, imaginative. His natural personality was affable and outgoing; he genuinely enjoyed people and got along with those of every social stratum. He was physically courageous, and unflappable in a dangerous situation. On three occasions in his agency career, he had killed—twice under pressure when operations had been bollixed or betrayed. In each instance he had revealed none of the hesitation of compunction that could get a man dead.

And yet, for the last five years of his service, this model agent had been exploiting his position and contacts to lay the foundation for his ultimate act of betrayal of his colleagues and country.

CIA psychologists had developed a theory to explain Edwards's actions. The world of espionage was incredibly complex, they pointed out. Double-cross, betrayal, and deception were everyday components of it, so that the line between ally and antagonist could change position almost daily. In addition, the individual agent was only one small cog in the great intelligence machine; often it became difficult for the agent to relate the purpose of his operations to the greater scheme of his nation's interest.

As a psychological defense, even a competent and loyal agent perceived his work as an exercise in logistics and intellect. Accepting as a given fact that he was working on the right side, he would then bring nothing but a cold precision to his operations.

There was nothing wrong with this, the psychologists pointed out. It was mentally healthy and stable, and served the agency's best interests. It became dangerous only when it was carried one step further, as Frank Edwards had done.

Edwards had rejected completely the link between his intelligence activities and the greater good. Sure, he understood that as an agent of the CIA he was promoting the interests of the United States; it was just that he had decided that those interests no longer had anything to do with him. The operation—the game—became an end in itself.

From there, the decision to operate solely in one's own behalf was not a large step.

"It would be erroneous," one CIA psychologist

wrote, "to diagnose Edwards as mentally unhealthy. On the contrary, from a purely logical point of view, Edwards's behavior is entirely rational."

Rational, maybe. But Bolan knew that the world does not revolve upon an axis of rationality. To co-exist, people had to accept and embrace emotion as well—emotions like loyalty, commitment to something of worth, moral vision.

Instead, Frank Edwards had chosen a life of ethical vacancy, a commitment only to power and wealth with no thought whatsoever to those at whose expense he would prosper.

It was a hollow world that Frank Edwards had created for himself.

And Mack Bolan meant to pop it open.

17

The chronometer on Bolan's left wrist read 0730:00, Tripoli time.

Twisting the arm far enough to see it sent a faint ripple of hurt across the left side of his chest. It was another reminder that he would have to compensate for the less-than-full use of that arm. Everything had to go down exactly on the numbers, and there were no numbers to spare. This hit had to take out Edwards, but it would still have to be as soft as possible. Call it semisoft.

Call it the end of a traitor's megalomaniacal master plan.

The middle-aged guard Bolan had seen occupying the gatehouse at Edwards's Giorgimpopoli villa a couple of hours earlier had gone off duty. His replacement was a younger man, a swarthy Berber in the same immaculate livery. The Berber listened to the name Bolan gave him, picked up a phone, repeated the name into it, then after a pause nodded Bolan on up the curving driveway.

Like he'd figured, the gateman was more for show than anything else. The hard security began at the front door.

Bolan pulled the Jag up to the villa. A couple of

other cars were already there, two sleek black limos. Edwards was giving his guests the red-carpet treatment.

Bolan had another treatment in mind for Edwards.

The doorman wore a neatly pressed green jump suit without insignia of any kind, and a Colt .45 automatic in a web-belt supported holster on his left hip. He was an American. According to Toby, there were three or four other hardmen besides him at the villa, also from the U.S. It could have been a glimmer of chauvinism on Edwards's part, or more likely just the practical knowledge that he could find no better trained personnel anywhere. In this case, the four were all one-time Special Forces, recruited by T.W. Hansen, the one-time master sergeant whose brain fluids were now watering the grassy plain near Wheelus Air Base. They were tough, competent hardmen, combat-experienced, who had sold their deadly skills to the renegade agent.

"Sid Bryant," Bolan announced to the guy as he got out of the Jaguar.

"May I have your card please, Mr. Bryant."

Bolan got out the wallet he had appropriated from Bryant. The slip he extracted was the size of a business card, with a series of random symbols—a dollar sign, an ampersand, a star—printed across it. The doorman tore off one corner; the card was made of three plies of different colored paper, like a tote ticket at a parimutuel horse-racing track. Like most of the more simple applications of tradecraft, it was effective. To counterfeit the card that identified the bearer, you not only had to know the order of the

symbols, but the order and color of the card's plies—
and Edwards could change either at will.

The doorman examined the torn corner, looked
satisfied. Then he gave Bolan the once-over, his gaze
pointedly lingering on the area of Bolan's left armpit.

"Are you carrying a gun, Mr. Bryant?" the guard
said neutrally.

"That's right," Bolan said pleasantly. He had
donned a light jacket over the khaki safari shirt.
Beneath it gun-leather held a compact Beretta 92S
autoloading pistol.

"May I have it please?"

"Nope," Bolan said, just as pleasantly. "I feel
naked without it."

The guard frowned.

"Look," Bolan went on seriously, "I'm walking
into a place I've never been before. You get me to
Edwards, and him and me will talk about my gun. I
won't shoot anyone before that."

The guard didn't like that, but Bryant was a guest.
He opened the lid of a recessed box set into the door
jamb and spoke. Footsteps sounded inside, and the
doorman opened up. Two other men, dressed and
armed like the guy on the door, were coming down
the hall. One was dark-haired, slim, and very tall—
six-eight or -nine, Bolan guessed. The other was redheaded and burly.

"He's heeled," the doorman told them.

The redhead nodded blankly. "This way, Bryant."

He took the lead, followed by Bolan, the very tall
guy bringing up the rear, Indian-file style. The villa
was cool, dim, elegant, and decorated in a vaguely

European style. The furniture Bolan could see was soft and plush, leather-covered cushions on solid hardwood chassis. They went down a long hall, as Bolan called into mind the detailed sketches of the place Toby had worked up, etching the layout into his consciousness.

They passed sliding oak double doors on the left, which would open into a chandeliered dining room. On either side were oil paintings that looked like originals, framed in gilded hand-carved mountings. The hall ended in a carpeted double-wide staircase; at the top they turned and went back toward the front of the house, passing almost a dozen closed doors on either side of the second-story passageway.

At its end the redheaded bodycock knocked on the last door. Above it was a motor-mounted video camera. The door swung open.

Bolan's mind registered more leather-covered furniture; a monitor for the video camera set in the wall above the door; a small conference table with chairs; the two side walls covered with floor-to-ceiling shelves lined with mostly leather-bound volumes. The opposite wall was almost all window, shaded by semi-opaque draperies through which some of the early-morning sunshine filtered. In front of the draperies was a hardwood desk, its flat top as big as a bench, as baroquely styled as the rest of the house's furnishings.

Frank Edwards sat behind the desk.

He nodded, said, "Hello, Bryant," and stood up.

Physically, he was not especially impressive. He was two or three inches shorter than Bolan's six feet,

and had a pleasant open face and conservatively cut
dark hair that was beginning to thin in front. He had
the kind of compact stocky build that, when dressed
in well-cut clothing, could have been either muscled
or gone slightly to fat. Bolan could not be sure,
because the clothes he wore were extremely well cut:
a charcoal-gray summer-weight suit, a pale shirt, a
plainly striped rep tie. A watch with a gold expansion
bracelet circled his wrist.

The result was quiet wealth without ostentation.
Edwards could have been an executive of a multinational corporation, or even a statesman.

In a way he was a corporate president. His product
was a full line of accessories for the well-equipped
terrorist everywhere.

And he didn't need either of his hardboys to pass
on the doorkeeper's observation. "Would you mind
giving up your side arm to one of my men for the
time being, Bryant?"

"Yeah," Bolan said, "I'd mind."

"Look, Bryant, this is supposed to be a get-
acquainted visit. We're both pros. You know how
this has to go."

Nothing had changed in the guy's stance, expression, or tone, but somehow he was suddenly project-
ing a chill. It was the eyes, Bolan realized. They were
dark, steady, cold as gunmetal. In contrast to the
persona the man's clothing presented, his eyes gave
off nothing at all.

If eyes were the mirror of the soul, Frank Edwards
was soulless.

Bolan shrugged and fished out the Beretta with

two fingers. He laid it on Edwards's desk, and watched the man frown at the ugly snout of the automatic's silencer.

"I don't like loud noises," Bolan said.

The whole role camouflage was carefully contrived to present a specific image. Bolan's version of Sid Bryant was of a tough, self-assured agent—but one a little too glib, a little too pushy. He wanted Edwards to feel superior to Bryant, and to lose a few shavings of alertness for that reason.

As for the Beretta, it had already played its primary role, which was not unlike the florid gestures a stage magician uses to misdirect his audience. The wrangle over its surrender had forestalled a full body-search—and had in point of fact *not* left Bolan unarmed.

The guard who had been inside the office when they arrived watched Bolan narrowly. His name, according to Toby, was Kenneth Briggs, and he was Edwards's personal bodycock, on him always, like a secret service man on the president. That made him Edwards's choice as the best man.

Bolan returned the gaze. He would accept Edwards's opinion and treat the guy with appropriate caution.

"I have some people downstairs," Edwards said. "A breakfast meeting I'd already planned before we got in contact. It will take an hour or so. I'd like you to wait up here." His tone left no room for argument. But then Bolan hadn't intended any.

"Boyd and Whiston will stay with you." Edwards smiled very slightly. "For company." He came around the desk, headed for the office door. "I'll have breakfast sent up."

"Thanks," Bolan said dryly.

Edwards went out, tagged by Briggs.

Based on what Toby had told him, Bolan had come into this on-the-edge soft penetration armed with a few knowns. Known: Edwards had a breakfast meeting with four bad-egg agents from the Red side of the fence. Known: Edwards's guard contingent at this softsite was four or five very tough men. Known: a computer terminal, phone-linked to the mainframe at Wheelus and manned by a technician, was located in one of the second-story rooms. Known: communication with Wheelus was maintained by land-line and two-way radio both.

From the knowns had come the assumptions. Assumption: Edwards was hardly going to invite Bolan to join the breakfast meeting. Assumption: Bolan would be guarded, and guarded well.

From all of that, Bolan had fashioned his plan. The framework went by the numbers, but the fleshing out allowed for the likely necessity of playing by the ear at some point.

The difficulty came from the mission's dual goals—neutralize Edwards, and wipe out his Wheelus base. To accomplish both, without one site tipping off the other as soon as the play began, was where the numbers got sticky.

Bolan would almost have to be in two places at once.

That was impossible. But many times in the past when he had faced the impossible, Bolan had simply substituted the improbable.

"Let's go, Bryant," Boyd, the carrottop, said. He stood, picked up Bolan's Beretta, and stuck it in the front of his belt.

"Where we going?"

"Just follow me."

Two doors down the hall, Boyd unlocked a door and let Bolan precede him and Whiston in. The Old World elegance of the villa ended at the threshold. The room was windowless, painted all white. Louvered fluorescent light fixtures were set into the ceiling; in opposite corners video cameras behind wire-mesh cages swept the entire room. The only furniture was a plain wooden table and four straight-backed wooden chairs. The door they came through was nearly a foot thick and whispered precisely shut; Bolan assumed it, and the rest of the room, was soundproof.

It was a multipurpose room, and none of its purpose had much to do with the gentility radiated by the rest of the house. This space was built for imprisonment, interrogation, isolation, and torture, if it came to that.

Whiston took one of the chairs, set it next to the door, and folded his long frame to straddle it backward. Boyd gestured Bolan toward one of the others.

"I'm not so sure I like the way this is going," Bolan said. He put on a cocky grin and let a wash of fear show through it. "I guess I'll be running along."

"What is this, amateur hour?" Boyd said.

Whiston snorted.

Bolan lit a cigarette with a Zippo lighter. "So," he said through a cloud of smoke. "You boys like your work?"

"No smoking."

"Is that so?" Bolan said, still cocky.

"Look," Boyd said reasonably. "The ventilation in here is lousy."

"So let's go someplace else."

Boyd leaned across the table, both palms flat on it. "Listen, Bryant."

Bolan held his right arm straight out from the side, let the butt drop to the white floor, all the while staring defiantly into Boyd's gaze.

"That's it, smart guy... "

"Okay, okay," Bolan said quickly. He bent under the table after the butt.

He swept up the leg of the twill slacks with his left hand, and the little C.O.P. .357 Magnum leaped from the ankle holster into his good right.

Boyd was sharp enough to catch the import of the motion and realize he was in a vulnerable position in the same instant. Instead of jumping back, he put his weight into the table, tried to topple it on Bolan.

Bolan ducked under it, hit the redheaded hardman in the knees. Boyd took a step back, blocking out Whiston, but did not go down. The muzzle of his Colt .45 cleared leather.

Bolan shot him in the chest at a range of three feet.

The explosion of the heavy-caliber round in the soundproof room was loud enough to be painful— but not as painful as the slug. Boyd bucked into the air, spun half around to show a ragged exit wound in the middle of his backbone, nearly crashed into Whiston.

Straddling the chair had not been a good idea. The

second hardman learned that a moment too late—and took the lesson to eternity with him. He was trying to draw, stand, and avoid Boyd's body all at once, and he had finished none of the motions when the C.O.P. boomed again and most of his chin and jaw caved into his face as he flew off the chair, all arms and long legs.

Bolan got to his feet, not without pain. As he had rolled, a wrenching bolt had tormented his left shoulder and chest. He could feel wetness seeping into the fresh compress he had applied when he dressed in the Bryant camouflage. With much more punishment he would not be able to control the arm at all.

He retrieved the silenced Beretta from Boyd's belt, wiping flecks of blood off its butt on the dead man's blouse. The 92S went back where it belonged. From Boyd's trouser pocket he took the key to the white room.

As he straightened, someone knocked on the door.

Bolan palmed the little .357 inside his jacket pocket, then eased open the door a crack. A young Arab in some kind of servant uniform was holding a tray with three cups, a coffeepot, and a covered dish.

"He say bring up breakfast." His accent was thick, and his tone seemed sullen, as if he resented the job or any other.

But neither his attitude nor the fact he was Arab made him a terrorist. He could have been just what he looked like: a servant who'd had a fight with his wife that morning before coming to work.

Bolan was not about to harm the guy on suspicion—but he couldn't let him run loose either.

Bolan opened the door wide enough to slip through. "In there," he told the guy. The Arab scowled and went past him into the white room.

The door sighed shut in time to cut off the crash of the tray hitting the floor, and the guy's strangled gasp of fear and surprise.

Bolan locked the door, pocketed the key, and moved on down the hall.

18

There were other keys on Boyd's ring, but Bolan did not waste time trying them. The Beretta whispered, and wood cracked. Holding the silenced gun up and ready, Bolan put the flat of his foot against the door at the far end of the hall from Edwards's office.

The room was a bedroom, a guest room from the unoccupied looks of it. Bolan waited a moment, every sense alert, then crossed past a door opening into a bathroom, and on to a glass-and-lattice door.

This one was unlocked. Bolan stepped out onto a balcony facing off the rear corner of the building. Below him, the back of the villa's grounds continued the Old World European theme. There was a circular formal garden, cut into fourths by paths that led to a gazebo at its center. The gazebo was surrounded by a shallow moat that served as a fish pond; delicately arched foot-bridges connected it with the paths.

To maintain this landscaping, to pipe in the de-salinated water—precious as wine in this country—needed for irrigation would be fabulously expensive. It was yet another emblem of Edwards's success at his chosen profession.

The profession of betrayal.

Now, the bill for all his lovely things was going to come due.

Bolan quickscanned the grounds, but there was no one out yet at this early hour. Above, at the corner of the house, was a junction box where electric and telephone wires, mostly hidden along their path by the upper branches of strategically planted trees, came into the villa.

From his inside pocket Bolan took a foil-wrapped rectangle the size and shape of a pack of cigarettes. Inside was a block of plastique explosive into which a mechanical spring-wound clock mechanism had been pre-embedded. He made it up on top of the balcony railing, holding the electric conduit for balance, keeping his left arm as close to his injured side as possible.

But when he tried to reach up to place the plastique in position, even though he used his right arm, the wound screamed white-hot pain in protest.

His mobility was deteriorating rapidly. The right was supposed to be unaffected, but perhaps the muscle tear had worsened under all the activity. The arm was extended only three-quarters of full, but that seemed to be its limit.

The junction box was six inches farther up.

Clutching the conduit with the left, Bolan rose on his toes. That yielded another three inches—and another brilliant explosion of hurt.

Sweat dappled his forehead. Bolan gritted his teeth and reached.

He closed his eyes instinctively against the tears of pain, molding the little brick of explosive to the bottom of the junction box by touch. By the time he was able to drop the arm and get back down to the balcony itself, he was breathing as hard as if he had just run a five-minute mile.

Inside the empty bedroom, he gave himself a few beats of closed-eyed rest, breathing deeply but with control, willing the pain to lessen.

By then it was time to move out again.

When Bolan came through the door of the communications room, a white-coated balding man seated at a console spun around in his swivel chair, his eyes wide.

He wasn't alone.

There was a guard there, dressed like the others, but he was faster. His gun was already out and coming up.

Bolan was faster still. The Beretta spoke a soft word, and blood bloomed on the front of the guy's blouse as he slammed back against the wall and slumped to the floor, suddenly unseeing eyes staring witlessly at his Executioner.

"The personnel file," Bolan said in a flat steely voice. "I want it."

The bald technician did not move. Saliva flicked his trembling lips.

Bolan crossed the room, let the guy look into the blackness of the Beretta's silencer.

"The names of the ones who have signed on with Edwards. Now."

This one was by the ear, yet again, but it was a short-odds gamble. Bolan was counting on Edwards's training and his affinity for hi-tech methods.

They would dictate that records be kept, and the logical place for keeping them was in Edwards's mainframe computer at the Wheelus base. And according to Toby, it was tied in by phone link to the villa.

Bolan lay the muzzle against the guy's high bald forehead.

"I...I...."

"Do it," Bolan said softly.

The guy spun around in his chair. It took him a moment to get his trembling fingers under control. He tapped at a keyboard, moaned as he made an error. The video display in front of him went blank as he started over.

A moment later a line printer in the corner started to chatter out copy.

Bolan went over and glanced at it as it came up.

It was all there: names, code names, aliases, service histories, affiliations, contracts. Nearly two dozen agents, some still active, some terminated for a variety of real and contrived reasons. Among them they represented every major country, free and communist, in the world.

Bolan ripped off the printout, folded it and stuffed it in his jacket pocket. It was not his function to interfere in the workings of the intelligence services of other nations, but he would pass the list along, for sure. A lot of directors were going to be unpleasantly surprised to find out that some of their key people had traded loyalty for avarice. But they'd also be damned relieved to find out who they were.

The precarious world balance would be that much more stabilized.

A lot of bad apples were going to be shaken out of the tree.

Next to the line printer was a radio transceiver. Bolan put three 9mm slugs into its face.

The balding technician was staring at him, gap-mouthed.

"Turn around," Bolan ordered.

The guy looked at the dead roomguard. Most of his upper torso was now greasy with blood. The guy began to sob, as if he had seen a vision of his destiny revealed.

"Turn around," Bolan said again.

The blubbering guy slowly put his back to Bolan. Bolan hit him behind the ear, just hard enough to stop the blubbering.

He paused only long enough to reassure himself that the guy's pulse and breathing were steady, before following the declining numbers out of the room.

He did not want to be late for breakfast.

The waiter wheeling the serving cart looked up at Bolan in surprise. Then he saw the Beretta, and the surprise turned to fright.

In front of the cart were the double doors to the dining room. Bolan flattened himself against the wall to one side, gestured to the waiter with the pistol.

The waiter slid the doors to either side and rolled the cart inside.

Bolan spun around behind him, tracked down the Beretta, and said, "You're first, Edwards."

He was counting on the other man's documented coolness under fire. For the moment it worked.

"Don't anyone move," Edwards said softly.

In all there were five men around the table. Edwards sat at the head. Bolan recognized the others from Toby's description. The two on Edwards's right hand were senior agents of the Russian KGB. Across from them was a colonel in the Cuban *Dirección General de Inteligencia*, and a ranking officer of the extremist Popular Front for the Liberation of Palestine. In front of each was the rind from a crescent of melon.

"Hands flat on the table," the Man from Ice ordered.

"Do what he says," Edwards echoed. "None of you are in any danger in this house."

They were free to believe that if they wished. In fact, Bolan did not consider any of them as targets, unless it was their lives or his. Sure, they were enemies of everything Bolan cherished, but no war had been declared. Though Bolan might rue the fact, he knew that along with the official sanction he had accepted came limitations, restraints.

Five pairs of arms framed the melon plates.

Though he contained it, Bolan's righteous anger gnawed at him. These four were not renegades, not in the sense that Edwards was. Possibly they were here on their own initiatives; but just as possibly they were present on direct sanction of the governments they represented. It was common and confirmed knowledge that the Soviet Union and its client states were semi-supporters of international terrorism. Edwards's scheme would undoubtedly accrue to their benefits as well, and perhaps even attract their covert support.

"What do you want?" Edwards said calmly, in the same tone he might use to offer more coffee.

Bolan gave him no response but the implacable cold stare on which he had the guy skewered.

There were two other men in the room, besides the waiter, who had retreated to a corner to cower. Kenneth Briggs, Edwards's full-time bodycock, stood behind his boss, his hands up at shoulder level, palms out. A Slavic-featured guy in an ill-fitting suit that was too heavy for the climate stood behind the two KGB agents.

Bolan kept Briggs within the field of his peripheral vision. "Take the gun out and drop it," he told the guy. "Two fingers will do the job."

The heavy .45 thudded on the thick carpet.

Briggs was the dangerous one. Toby had managed to cozy up to the head bodycock once, get him talking. Before he had gone bad he had won nearly every decoration in the manual. And his two consecutive tours in Nam had been under jungle foliage, not a tin roof.

Like Bolan, Briggs was a survivor.

"Against the far wall," Bolan told the men at the table. "Your backs to me. Keep your hands high and make sure I can see them. Not you, Edwards."

The four men were professionals—pro enough to recognize walking death when they saw it. None of them made any abrupt moves as chairs slid away from the table.

Except for Briggs.

The big man picked the moment for its distraction, his right hand flashing behind his neck and out again, the movement smooth as an athlete.

And if Bolan had in fact been distracted, it might have worked.

Bolan twisted sideways, dropped to a crouch. There was no time for anything but a body shot. It was enough. The 9mm flesh-mangler caught Briggs in the middle of his flat stomach.

Behind Bolan the razor-sharp six-inch blade of the throwing knife quivered in the rococo woodwork.

Briggs sat down hard. Blood bubbled from his mouth. Then he seemed to shudder, and his eyes closed as he toppled over to sprawl across the carpet, no movement of breath disturbing his perfect stillness.

Bolan tracked onto the Russian bodycock and snapped, "Go ahead. But do it real slow."

The Russian's left hand came back out from beneath the lapel of his suit, gingerly holding a 9mm stockless Stechkin machine pistol. He let it drop.

Frank Edwards looked thoughtfully at the backs of the five men lined up against the wall across the table from Bolan. "Let me make a suggestion."

The man's tone was normal, conversational. But to Bolan it grated like fingernails on a chalkboard.

"I know who you are," Edwards went on. "Not your name, of course, but names don't mean that much." His open face broadened in a faint smile. "I hear things. About one man, doing a lot of damage to some of the people I, ah, associate with. In Panama, Turkey, across the frontier in Algeria."

Edwards shifted very slightly in his chair. Bolan's grip on the Beretta tightened. The trigger yielded to soft pressure.

"Hold on," Edwards said, his voice rising almost imperceptibly. "I could use someone like you."

Edwards drummed two fingers on his fine linen tablecloth. "It's a business, friend. It's nothing but a business."

Bolan stared at the guy. Over the length of his warrior years, he had pitted himself against many men. All of the enemy shared certain demonic qualities: a rapacious capability for self-enrichment and -aggrandizement; a callous and selfish disregard for the rights of anyone else; a slavish devotion to the subjugation and control of whoever dared stand in the way; and a willingness, even an eagerness, to adopt the most brutally violent expedients for attaining their objectives.

The Mafioso was a clannish beast, mobbing up to form a group strong enough to become the oppressor, because deep in his subconsciously held inferiority he knew that if he did not, he would become the oppressed. The terrorist professed to be driven by a greater cause, but neglected to inform you that the cause was generally a totalitarian regime of pure horror.

And then there was Frank Edwards.

Here was a man who professed no ideology at all, who took pride in his aloofness from the affairs of men and the fact that he sold his goods and services to any comer with the necessary cash. So what if the M-16 he sold would be used by some Palestinian maniac to spray a stream of 5.56mm death into a roomful of the elderly inhabitants of a Jewish nursing home in Germany? What was it to Edwards if he provided information enabling the kidnapping—and, after the ransom was paid, the execution—of an American executive whose only "crime" was to be a successful businessman? Why concern himself if a letter-bomb from his inventory blew up in the hands of a conservative British member of parliament?

Edwards claimed to be simply a private business-man serving a need. In fact, he was morally anes-thesized, a scavenger who renounced by his actions any kinship with the rest of human society. He was a parasite, sucking at the blood that terror spilled.

"Think about it, friend," Edwards said now. "Think about what I could do for you."

The man was a traitor. He had turned his back on ideals long before. All the years he had worked for his country, he had been storing away the knowledge and skills he'd picked up, to use against that country. When he had learned enough, he'd discarded his homeland like a pail of overripe garbage.

The treasonous bastard's very existence was an af-front to every notion of human decency.

"Power, wealth, you name it," Edwards offered. "Whatever you want."

"I've got what I want," the voice of death pro-nounced. "I've got you."

Yet the law could not touch Frank Edwards. The rules that man had made to ensure order and justice were essential to that balance that Bolan walked the tightrope to preserve. But like any compromise they were not perfect.

That was why Mack Bolan had chosen not to judge.

Long ago, he had chosen to act.

"You see how it is," Frank Edwards smiled.

Bolan's caress of the Beretta's trigger became an embrace.

The 9mm brain-scrambler plowed into the bridge of Edwards's nose, and the guy's face seemed to fold inward upon itself, the eyes drawing into each other and descending further into a glistening wetness of bone and blood and brain. The chair catapulted over, and Edwards flipped backward limply like the straw man he was and lay facedown, his life-essence turned to gore pooling in the deep nap of the carpet.

None of the five men at the wall moved a muscle.

Bolan dug the ring out of his pocket, wrenched off the key to the communications room. He tossed it into the lap of the cowering waiter.

"It fits one of the rooms upstairs." He tried to modulate his voice, but it came out a ragged rasp. "Use it."

The waiter stared down at the key like it was a live grenade, and he was paralyzed.

From toward the back of the house came the muffled explosion of the plastique. The lights of the chandelier blinked out. The junction box was gone.

The doorman was halfway down the hall, .45 in hand, when Bolan came out of the dining room. Bolan fired twice, and the doorman slid to the floor.

Bolan stepped over him and out into the early-morning sunshine. He divided the remaining rounds in the Beretta between the passenger-side windows of the two limousines, using the barrel to punch out the shattered glass.

From a satchel under the front seat of the Jaguar he took two HE grenades. He started the sedan, eased up beside the limos just long enough to pull pins, deposit the armed cans.

He was almost to the gate when the two vehicles went up in a swirling fountain of flame and twisted metal. The Berber guard's sullen expression turned to incredulity.

Bolan slewed out onto the street and pointed the Jag away from there.

19

Bolan was actually slightly ahead of the numbers as he pulled the Jag to the side of the straight two-lane blacktop access road to Wheelus. In the scrub grass to either side lay the wreckage of the boxy Mercedes and the sleek Saab Turbo, along with the bodies of the men who had been taking Toby Ranger on her last long ride.

He slid out from behind the wheel, opened the trunk, and began to rig for hard combat.

The fashionable threads that had been part of the Sid Bryant role camouflage were doffed. Underneath the compress, the twin punctures in his shoulder were an angry red. Bolan squeezed on more antibiotic salve, rebandaged them.

He could no longer move the left arm more than a few inches away from his side before the pain's protest overcame free will. From here on he was essentially a one-armed fighter; even pulling on the blacksuit became too difficult for the expenditure of the energy required. Bolan used the Fairbairon stiletto to cut off the suit's left sleeve, slitting down the left side to the waist. After that he was able to struggle into it.

The customized Beretta 93R machine pistol nestled

in leather on his right hip, primed for one-handed firing. The powerful little Uzi hung from a lanyard around his neck. Bolan could not afford to be without full-automatic fire capability, and though it cost him more pain, he found when he experimented that he could get his left arm out far enough to support the submachine gun's barrel. He seated an L-shaped double magazine in the well and charged the weapon. Extra speed-loaders, as well as an assortment of grenades and other small armament, went into the utility belt. In a specially designed case on his left hip were the Litton Night Vision Goggles.

He was patting down the suit, rechecking and memorizing positions and placements, when the sound of approaching vehicles came from beyond the rise that hid him from the Wheelus gate. Bolan slid back inside the Jag.

There were two of them, a 15-seater Mercedes minibus and a square-bodied Rover with two people up front, four passengers facing each other on the rear benches. Slumped in the Jag, Bolan caught glimpses of figures, faces. He saw mechanics' coveralls, white lab coats, well-worn American-style baseball caps. No one gave more than a passing glance at the Jag or the two wrecks in the field. The faces were etched with fear of what had just been left behind, and concentration on getting as far away as possible, as quickly as they could.

These were the noncombatants, routed moments earlier by Toby, sent fleeing into the glare of the early-morning sunshine. Judging from their expressions, Toby had convinced them beyond doubt that they did not want to be caught in the firestorm about to come. They were the scientists, the mechanics, the hi-tech gurus—the wizards of the arcane lore that was at the heart of Edwards's grand scheme.

Perhaps, Bolan contemplated, the world was becoming a technocracy, a society managed by the technical experts. Certainly the indications were there. They existed on the personal level, in the form of television systems allowing the viewer to talk back, or banks replaced by machines that swallowed or spewed out cash. It was just another way of hamstringing people's capability for direct action, by distancing them. Communication with or through a machine was not really communication; it was conveyance.

The technocrats held far greater power than that, however. They were at the heart of the systems of defense and destruction that lay poised and ready in the bowels of the supernations. For now they were at the fulcrum of the cosmic equilibrium. But if the technocrats overstepped their mandate, or miscalculated in any of a dozen different ways, the result could easily be a holocaust.

Without the technocrats, Frank Edwards would have been just another petty international hood.

The technological corps of Edwards's army of the night was hardly composed of innocents. If these people were intelligent enough to run Edwards's computer banks, communications net, and other state-of-the-art support equipment, they were intelligent enough to at least divine an inkling of what was going down. But intelligence and insight were two different things, and like many men of hard scientific knowledge, Edwards's people could be highly prone to the old forest-vs.-trees shortsightedness.

And there were relative degrees of guilt. These were not gun-toting hardmen who had turned their back on the country that had nurtured them. They were not fanatical terrorists to whom murder was as impersonal as life. Sure, indirectly their activities supported these types. But Bolan could not expect to eliminate, on suspicion only, every person who was vaguely tainted by the stink of terrorism.

Maybe the lesson of what was about to come down would impress itself upon these people. In any case they would not have their hi-tech toys to play with anymore.

This was the essential weakness of a technocracy: destroy its technology, and you bring the society to its knees.

That was Bolan's immediate objective.

There would still be men on the base, according to Toby's intelligence. At any given time, two to three dozen of the iron-hard inner circle were billeted at Wheelus. As at the Valais chalet, the guards were all active members of terrorist organizations, selected for their demonstrated commitment to violent propagation of "the cause." They were chosen to go to the base for various reasons: to select and purchase weapons, to maintain contact with other groups in the terrorist network, to receive advanced training from Edwards or his handpicked associates in sabotage, espionage, assassination, guerilla fighting, and all the rest of the black arts. In exchange for this,

they served tours as base guards. The largest and
hardest contingent was assigned to the armory where
Edwards's stock of illegally exported weaponry was
stockpiled. Every precaution was taken, for here was
the source of Edwards's immediate wealth, the finan-
cial base for much of his operation.

Unlike the technologists, these men fell into no
"gray" area. They were pure black, dedicating their
lives—willing even to sacrifice them, in some
fanatical cases—to their so-called "ideals."

If anything about repression, intolerance, persecution, subjugation, and domination could be called
"ideal."

Bolan rose in the seat as the Mercedes minibus,
and the Rover rumbled on by. Maybe some day the
technocrats would realize they were their own worst
enemy.

As for the terrorists, the lesson would be more immediate, more direct, and far more deadly.

Bolan keyed the ignition and the Jag rolled on toward the Wheelus base.

The electric gate eased open as he approached.
Bolan pulled to a stop at the guardhouse.

The contusion on Toby Ranger's forehead was
yellow and purple, and her face was pale and drawn.
When she opened the half-door of the guardhouse,
Bolan had a brief glimpse of the limp figure of the
regular guard, sprawled on the little structure's
floor.

Bolan slid over, and Toby got in behind the wheel.
Her eyes widened in inquiry when she saw the blacksuit's amputated sleeve.

"I'm all right," Bolan told her. He grinned. "If it doesn't fall off in the next ten minutes, we're home free." He was trying to take the edge off, but both of them had fought enough long-odds battles to know that ten minutes could pass in an eyewink—or stretch into a lifeless eternity.

"What about you?" Bolan asked.

"I'm...." She glanced back toward the guardhouse and unconsciously touched at the Colt .45 now strapped around the waist of the snug-cut white jump suit.

But when she turned back to Bolan her expression was set with resolution, and color was returning to her face. Bolan understood. If he did not know how many men had died at his hand, he did know that every kill had been personal. When his finger tightened on the trigger, no matter how great the necessity, no matter how evil the target, there was some recessed component of reluctance in Bolan's psyche.

A reminder that he was not, could not think of himself, as all-knowing, all-power. A reminder the man was human.

"I'm okay," Toby assured him, her voice strong and even. "Lead on, Captain Blitz."

Bolan checked his chronometer. "Eight forty-one forty," he said.

"One sec." Toby clicked at the button on her own matching timepiece.

"Eight forty-two," Bolan said. "Mark!"

"You got it." Toby slipped the Jag in gear and gave it gas.

A main drive bisected the old USAF base. To the

left was the primary aviation facility: maintenance shop, a terminal with control tower, then hangars, and beyond the buildings stretching across the flat concrete-covered plain, a maze of runways. To the right were the support structures: first some office buildings, and behind them a subdevelopment of billets, ranging from barracks to fairly nice homes that once housed married officers, now gone toward disrepair. After the billets came some stores, and then a couple of warehouses.

The last one housed the primary inventory of Frank Edwards's illicit weapons supply business.

But Toby turned the Jag to the left, heading for the hangar opposite the warehouse. She drove onto the apron. Parked down toward the terminal, Bolan spotted the Lear on which Bryant had arrived, along with a Beechcraft single-engine for local hops, and a surplus C-119 Flying Boxcar that had to be 30 years old. Sure, having your own cargo plane made good business sense, when you were dealing in the volume that Edwards was.

Toby steered the Jag around the end of the last hangar. There was a four-seater bubble-front helicopter in front of it, squatting on its skids.

Toby Ranger was already an IFR-licensed pilot in the days when she teamed with Bolan in Detroit. It was she who had flown the blitzing fighter north to Toronto to pursue one thread of the motor city investigation, and even in those days she was experienced and proficient with both the Lear and the Beechcraft. Since then, Bolan had been pleased to learn, she had added the chopper to her repertory.

The little rig's maneuverability would be an invaluable asset to the battle plan Bolan had worked out.

Within the shade of the hangar's wall, a guy was seated in the lotus position, his hands palm up in his lap. He wore a cap over dark hair, and khaki cutoff shorts, and he had a gut that hung over their waistline. The cap, the shorts, and the guy were all stained with motor oil. His eyes were closed, and he did not open them until Toby got out and slammed the Jag's door.

Toby nodded at the chopper. "Did you get her running, Buddha?"

The guy blinked at the sunlight. "Sure. Just a bearing in the tail rotor. She's runnin' good as new now." The guy's chatter ran down then; he had finally come out of his meditative trance enough to notice the .45 in Toby's hand. Bolan got out of the car, stood by its side but did not interfere.

"Gassed up?" Toby asked.

The guy she'd called Buddha—whether the nickname came from his meditative practices, or that godly gut, Bolan was not sure—stared at her. Toby repeated the question, a little more sharply. The guy nodded.

"Start her up, Buddha."

Bolan went into the shop, found a rag and a coil of insulated radio wire on a workbench. Behind him he heard the noise of the chopper's six-cylinder power plant starting up. A few moments later, Toby herded the fat guy into the dimness, and a few moments after that he was lying in a corner on his stomach, gagged and trussed like a turkey.

Bolan checked his chronometer and said, "Three minutes."

"Three it is, Captain Numbers," Toby said. "And counting." She reached out, touched his arm. "Be good," she said softly, "Captain Wonderful."

Be good, for sure.

Be good or be dead.

20

The armory was a windowless metal Quonset hut, the line of its ground-to-ground curved roof broken only by an oversized air-conditioning unit. Two khaki-clad Arabs flanked the door, automatic rifles with web belts slung over their shoulders.

Mack Bolan came around the corner of the hangar opposite. He paused just long enough to pull the Litton Night Vision Goggles into place, then floored the open jeep he had commandeered, aiming it at the two guys.

One of them managed to drop to his knee and sent a burst of autofire through the jeep's free-standing windshield. But by then Bolan had bailed out, coming down on his feet, rolling on his good shoulder.

The front of the jeep tore a ragged hole in the flat front end of the Quonset hut. Someone inside shouted.

One tire of the jeep was resting on the chest of the guy who had fired. His partner looked up from the other side, and Bolan's Beretta spit a silenced 9mm whizzer into his forehead.

Another guy threw open the door, gaped at the jeep, started to say, "What the hell...." The Beretta punched the rest of the words right back down his throat, and Bolan followed the body as it fell back inside the building.

A row of high-wattage bulbs ran along the spine of the curved ceiling. Bolan raised the Uzi and distributed a full 32-round magazine along that line, and the armory plunged into near-blackness, the only light trickling in from the rip the jeep had made in the wall.

Answering fire raked Bolan's position, muzzles flashing like stroboscopes in the darkness. But the man had moved on. His hands worked busily, dropped the clip from the Uzi, reversing it, seating it in the pistol-grip, racking back the cocking handle. His eyes scanned the cavernous room, everything clear as daylight through the NVD goggles, while other men shouted in anger and fear, waiting for their own eyes to adjust.

Crates of all sizes and descriptions were stacked on pallets, the pathways between them narrow canyons. In the canyon in front of Bolan, figures appeared. The Uzi chattered, its flash hidden, and four arms, four legs, two torsos fell into a tangled pile on the poured-concrete floor.

These men had reverted to the animals they were, the animal's primal fear of darkness and the unknown cutting at their confidence and effectiveness.

Now the dark warehouse was a pandemonium of shouting, cursing men groping toward the thin wash of light at Bolan's end of the building. Somewhere across the room an autorifle spoke, the muzzle flash directed away from Bolan. Someone screamed out pain, shot by his own side.

The Man from Hellfire stepped over the bodies

and into the inferno. The Uzi flamed its nine millimeters of firepower, and gut-reamers exploded through terrorist flesh. The man walked on, while savages suddenly visited by savagery of a new sort bellowed and bawled and bumped each other. Bolan sent them encouragement via the scream of the Uzi, the whisper of the sweet Beretta.

Other guns talked, but they accomplished nothing more than a revelation—a revelation answered by return fire that did not miss. Up and down the canyons behind the ceiling-high stacks of arms and other tools of the Savage, the man proceeded and his two guns talked.

At the end of an aisle, three wild-eyed candidates for another world scrambled into the open and found that world, when a sweeping burst of hollow-points tumbled through them to burst their torsos like ripe melons.

The man walked on, and the firestorm he left in his wake consumed only two of the allotted three minutes, followed by a moment of silence as profound as sleep. Yeah, the sleep of evermore.

Then, from outside, came shouts and gunfire and the distant whup-a-whup of the chopper's rotor.

The man found the crate he was looking for, ripped the top free. Inside were lengths of what might have been PVC piping—but was not. The man grabbed three lengths.

Then he turned back through the sickly sweet smell of fresh blood that mixed with the sharper acrid odor of gunpowder. His eyes were moving and alert, but he did not care to look over his handiwork.

The job was not quite over.

Another jeep with a tripod-mounted .50-caliber heavy machine gun on the open back deck was parked between the armory and the helicopter hangar. The gunner was hunched over, trying to fire the gun in an almost vertical line at the chopper hovering 100 feet above him. The jeep's driver was leaning back, holding the belt so it would not foul.

Bolan swept the Uzi from the belt-man to the gunner. The gunner's sudden deadweight dragged down on the trigger, and the big machine gun went on spitting harmless slugs into the air until the belt jammed.

Dust swirled as Toby set the chopper down in front of Bolan.

Another jeep was barreling down the street toward the helicopter. Bolan dropped to one knee, emptied the rest of the Uzi's magazine into the front of the hurtling rig. For a moment it neither slowed nor changed course.

Then, less than fifty feet distant, the jeep swerved to the left at an impossibly sharp angle. It flipped into the air. As Bolan dived into the copter's cockpit, he had a visual flash of a body cartwheeling through the air, arms and legs outflung. When the jeep blew, he and Toby were still close enough to the ground to feel the leading edge of the shock waves.

Bolan slipped on his headset in time to hear her ask, "What now, Captain Fire?"

Somehow the adrenaline of the armory blitz had overcome the pain in Bolan's shoulder, but it returned with a vengeance as he slipped·into the gunnery harness anchored to the front passenger seat's frame.

The human resistance below had been broken, and the means to finish off the armory was in Bolan's hands. But he knew that it was not enough. No one— Edwards, Khaddafi, or anyone like them—would exploit this U.S. base again.

The mission would only be done when Bolan had wiped it off the face of the earth.

"The planes, Toby," Bolan said. "It's mop-up time."

Toby kicked the little bird into a side-slip, and they skimmed the top of the hangar before she pulled up, holding steady at 100 feet, just upwind from the big-bellied C-119 Flying Boxcar.

Bolan selected one of the Light Artillery Weapons he had liberated from Edwards's cache. He pulled the pins to expand the disposable fiberglass tube, raised the pop-up sights. His right foot groped out the door for the skid, found it, let it hold his weight, then he leaned farther out.

The gunnery harness would not reach.

Toby turned in time to see his hands working to free the buckles. "Oh, no, you don't," she snapped.

"I have to be completely clear of the cockpit," Bolan smiled tensely, "or the backburn will knock us out of the sky."

"You're hurt, Mack," she began to plead.

"Hold her steady," Bolan interrupted, then stripped off the headset.

He held the LAW in his right hand, grasped the doorframe with his left, ignored the wrenching pain. Then he was completely outside and dropping into a straddle on the skid, steadying himself against the fuselage in a last desperate demand that his body not betray him.

Bolan got the C-119 in the sights, squeezed out fire. The rocket whooshed away on a trail of flame, impacting in the midst of the transport's fat body. A moment later the fuel tanks went, the impact flipping the nearby Beechcraft onto its back, while a huge plate of the C-119's body metal sheared into the Lear.

Bolan stabbed a forefinger forward, and the copter eased in the direction indicated. Bolan leaned inside, snagged the second LAW.

This one bored in at the base of the control tower. The tower swayed like a redwood tree sawn three-quarters of the way through, then it toppled to the apron in a grinding dusty crash.

The chopper lifted skyward, skithering above the hangar.

Someone had re-manned the heavy chattergun. A line of .50 slugs punched across the chopper's tail.

Bolan ignored him as he sent home the third LAW round.

The rocket punched through the thin metal of the Quonset hut's roof near its middle.

A heartbeat later, the armory's contents began to blow.

A roiling pillar of fire erupted through the ceiling, great spouts of molten metal cascading into the air like a demonic fountain. Jagged strips of metal, giant in size, flew incredible distances. Waves of shock and heat banged across the base.

The effect was virtually thermonuclear.

Angry balls of flame roared into the billets and offices, some of them already bursting into spontaneous combustion. Across the wide street, hangar walls bent and buckled and distorted, and roofs sagged like Silly Putty before collapsing. The gunnery jeep exploded, throwing parts of the gunner into the madness.

And the few terrorists still alive were caught under the hellish downpour of white-hot liquid metal, volcanic spews of sheet-fire, charred chunks of human flesh.

Bolan let the LAW's disposable tube drop from his stiff fingers.

When he tried to climb back into the cockpit, he found he could not. Toby gaped at him in alarm, tried to reach across toward him. Bolan flashed her a hand signal. When she hesitated, he circled thumb and forefinger in an "okay" sign.

Even that was an effort.

She brought the chopper down well outside the perimeter fence, hovering a few feet over the grass to allow Bolan to slip to the ground.

He managed to get to his feet by himself. When Toby leaped from the cockpit, ducked around the chopper, and flew into his arms, he even managed to maintain his balance.

EPILOGUE

Maintaining the balance. That, in the world view, was what it was all about.

He had achieved it once again. For now.

Hell was not for the living, it was for the dead, may they rest in peace. Someday Mack Bolan, too, would rest. For now, he had to find his way among the living.

As had long ago been prophesied, The Executioner would live life to the very end.

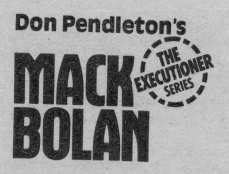

Don Pendleton's

MACK BOLAN

THE EXECUTIONER SERIES

JOHN PHOENIX RECLASSIFIED

"Call me clean as soon as possible," the printout had said.

"What's the hot, Hal?" Whatever it was, it was too hot for open circuits. "Don't tell me—April's dyed her hair blonde," Bolan chuckled into the mouthpiece. "That's what Carl Lyons told me once, you believe that?" His droll voice swelled into the clean connection.

'Striker, we're safing you," said the gruff voice of the Washington Wonderland man. "Listen to this. Let me read it to you:

"Re: Declassification—Problem has been retrieved without any loss of security. Has been in part reclassified. We will see no error from now."

Bolan said, "Fine, Hal," and killed the loop.

His wound was healing now, he was strong again. Hal's news about the rectifying of a recent apparent declassification stirred him.

So Bolan was in some ways back to what he used to be, the Mack Bolan who—in the official book—was once the largest criminal of all, the guy who would, in fact, have had it no other way.

From death master in Nam to a soldier—not a cop—in the war of the warrior with no army, to now, Stony Lonesome still. The loneliness of the Phoenix secret.

So, good. Fine.

It was a secret war once more.

The wildcat was back in the bag.

John Phoenix was free to hide.

Born of ashes, he had arisen on the wing, had now descended to earth in piercing hellrain, next to prowl like a winged panther over strange lands in *The Libya Connection*. So be it. Bolan was back, in the dark.

A good place to begin, if you seek the light.

Watch for *The Libya Connection*, Executioner #48, wherever paperback books are sold—December, 1982.

PHOENIX FORCE

AN Executioner SERIES

#3 Atlantic Scramble

ON SALE NOW!

The real Phoenix Force unleashed at last!

"Talk!" Katz spat in Arabic. "Where have you hidden the guns?"

"I don't know!" squealed the cornered killer.

"You lie!" Katz smashed him across the side of his face with the sharpened claws of his prosthetic hand. "Talk while you have a chance or I'll turn you over to *him*—" he indicated the wild-eyed McCarter, then the stony-faced Keio "—or *him*! They'll kill you by inches."

McCarter, in one swift stroke, brought up a haymaker that nearly tore the man's head off. He bore in for another shot but Yak waved him back. "Don't be greedy, David. Give somebody else a chance...!"

ABLE TEAM

#3 Texas Showdown
ON SALE NOW!

Bolan's three-man team strikes hot!

The nation needs good men, and in Carl Lyons, Pol Blancanales and Gadgets Schwarz the nation gets them, Bolan style. These are men who put forth both whispering death and screaming silvered fury!

In TEXAS SHOWDOWN, Able Team rips apart a billionnaire's plans for the invasion of Mexico. The Death-Squad-reborn blitzes its way to the hellheart of the drug wars, political sex wars—all-out war!

"For the spin-off novels, Don Pendleton has sought the expert collaboration of Dick Stivers for Able Team and Gar Wilson for Phoenix Force, both well versed in antiterrorist tactics and paramilitary matters, resulting in added realism and detail!"

—*Mystery News*